AF603936

Niño Paquito
Childhood tales

by Francisco Sáenz Ráez

NIÑO PAQUITO
Childhood tales

Edited by: Corporación Ígneo, S.A.C.
For its editorial seal Ediquid
Av. Arequipa 185 1380, Urb. Santa Beatriz. Lima, Perú
First edition, April, 2023

ISBN: 978-612-5078-85-8
Print run: 50
Legal Deposit in the National Library of Peru N° 2023-03037
Impression finished in April, 2023 at:

ALEPH IMPRESIONES SRL
Jr. Risso 580 Lince, Lima

www.grupoigneo.com
Email: contacto@grupoigneo.com
Facebook: Grupo Ígneo | Twitter: @editorialigneo | Instagram: @grupoigneo

Translation: Brad Holmes

Colection: Nuevas Voces

Contents

Dedication

For her giving me so much joy, insisting that I write these stories, and making me believe that they would be read, I dedicate these little gifts, these affectionate little jokes, to my daughter Daniela. For her sweet way of believing in me and infusing hope into my life, even when I felt it was running out.

To my daughters, Milagros, María Paz, and María Gracia, for my joy of living, for the peace they bring to my, at times afflicted, soul, and for being the miracles who inspire me.

To my wife for unwaveringly accompanying my uncertain steps and turning them into a fertile journey.

To my three mothers for their tender vigilance.

To my carnal and spiritual family.

To all who read to their grandchildren the brief contents of and affectionate substance of this book.

Acknowledgements

To my brothers and sisters for bringing me so much love and helping me to remember them.

To my mother Perpetua for sowing so much sweetness in my arid heart and allowing me to harvest something of sensitivity that can be transmitted.

To my friends for their presence during the days of my childhood and youth. Your experiences by my side comfort me and produce and bear the fruit which is to be shared.

To Manuel Rangel, my generous son-in-law, for listening to my stories over and over again, and escorting, without squeamishness or fussing, my slow procession.

Prologue

By José Luis González Martín
EDUCATIONAL PSYCHOLOGIST

The words of *Niño Paquito*, written and chiseled by Francisco Sáenz Ráez, allow us to create and make us feel the writer's art and the capacity for "empathy," through which we are able to understand other human beings, whether they are our relatives or friends, or are near or beyond the oceans; to understand, learn, and respect their different ways of life: their behaviors, their prejudices, their thoughts and expressions, their loves and emotions.

The "empathy" radiated by the stories and anecdotes in this book communicates to us through the people with whom, and the society in which, we are immersed. It also teaches us to, throughout our lives, work for a better, more sensitive, less bellicose, and more humane world.

The words of *Niño Paquito* create a reality that becomes incarnate, soothing our sentiments. Without wanting to, it nestles into a nook within our lives, becoming a reality that makes us laugh with those who laugh, suffer with those who suffer, love with those who love, and cry with those who cry.

The words of *Niño Paquito* beckon us to a place where we can absorb, little by little, drop by drop, that restorative silence of our lost illusions, of our unlived lives, and of everything that could have been and was not.

His words are scented with eucalyptus, strawberries, walnut trees, and black cherries; of white and full moons that graze across the sky with its infinite flocks of stars and heavenly bodies.

I believe that *Niño Paquito* is a complete rosary of anecdotes and experiences, held captive in sleep throughout the years in a weeping rain, in a field of green wheat, within a bell that tolls, in a love that the night has broken and that in the dawn of the new day, soaked in silence, awakens anew.

The *Niño Paquito* makes us think of a habitable, human reality, reaching to where the joy of forgiveness, the wisdom of justice, and the elation of love may be born in the hearts of the readers.

Preface

These short narratives are true stories and are written for people your age.

Young Paquito had three mothers, that's the truth. This boy had three mothers! If you don't believe it, ask your mother or your aunt if they knew Paquito. If not, if they didn't know him, by reading these stories, you will know him, you will know that it is true that he had three mothers and you will be able to tell others about it.

Mechita was the mother who gave birth to him, Mechita is the name of his first mother. She brought him into the world with father's help. His father's name was Gonzalo and he worked milking cows. His second mother's name was Delia, from the time she was a little girl she was called Delishita because she was very small and good. She was also called *Pasita*, because she was so tiny that she looked like a raisin, that is, a very small raisin. Do you know what a raisin is? A raisin is a very sweet, rich, and nutritious dried grape, and if it is very small it is called a *pasita*. Have you ever eaten raisins? Do you like raisins?

Raisins are always small because they have lost their water.

Delishita was Gonzalo's sister (don't forget that Gonzalo was Paquito's father)... I will take this opportunity to ask you some questions. What was the name of Paquito's first mother? What was the name of his second mother? What was Delia called?

Now I am going to ask you a more difficult question: if Gonzalo was Delishita's brother and Gonzalo was young Paquito's father, how were Paquito and Delishita related? Very good! Actually, Paquito was Delishita's nephew and she was Paquito's aunt.

Delishita was also Paquito's second mamita because she loved Paquito and his siblings like a mother. She helped Gonzalo and Mechita raise their twelve little children. Would you like to have eleven siblings? Do you think that's too many?

Years later Delishita adopted Paquito as her son. Do you know what it means to adopt? Do you know why some people adopt children? It's true, they adopt them to raise them. In this case it was to help raise Paquito, but the main reason to adopt a child is because that person loves him or her very much and the child also loves his or her adoptive mom or dad. Do you know someone who has an adopted child? Who he or she is? Do you know a child who has been adopted? Who he or she is? Do you think he or she is happy?

Paquito's third mamita was named Maria del Carmen (Maria in honor of the mother of Jesus of Carmen, or Carmen, because it means "God's paradise"), but they called her Perpetuita. Perpetua is a name, and from that comes the diminutive Perpetuita, which means little Perpetua or a very beloved Perpetua.

Perpetuita is a term of endearment, the diminutive of Perpetua, which means eternal or most lasting. Maria del Carmen was called Perpetuita because she was very consistent, because she was true and would last forever. Her love would be perpetual, this means that Perpetuita's love would be quite long, very long lasting, eternal, forever.

Would you like to have a perpetual love, a love that lasts forever? Do you think you could love someone forever? Ask the person reading this if he or she will love you forever.

Paquito had eleven siblings, so Perpetuita also helped raise Paquito. His mother Mechita had a lot of work with so many children. They were all obedient, but they all had to be fed, groomed, and dressed. So Perpetuita was the third mother of Paquito and his siblings.

Why was Perpetuita Paquito's third mother? Would you like to have three mothers?

The three mommies, Mechita, Delishita, and Perpetuita, helped each other and raised the twelve little brothers and sisters. They would all have to be very obedient, don't you think? Fortunately, all the children were not the same age; when the youngest, named Kiko, was born, Paquito was already 15 years old. Paquito was a very naughty boy, according to his mother Mechita; very smart, according to his mother Delishita, and very good, according to his mother Perpetuita.

This book of stories is told to you by Paquito and I, according to what we saw and according to what he lived or what he was told. Paquito and I hope you like them.

We wrote this book for your enjoyment and, especially, to spark the memory of those who lived through those times and remember the people and places described herein.

This preface is written in a childish way, but what we say below is addressed to you, the reader, whether you are fond of memories or passionate about reading about matters of the soul. After all, as Antione de Saint–Exupery pointed out in his book "The Little Prince:"

"All older people have begun by being children (although few remember it)."

As a means of clarification

Due to the diversity of characters that inhabit this book of stories, a descriptive list describing each one has been created. If you find yourself confused with the names of any of them or find it difficult to identify who is who, we suggest you go to the last section, which is at the end of this book, where there is an explanation of the identity of each character.

Translator's note

The translator's job, obviously, is to make the author's words and ideas fully understandable in the language of the targeted readership. This requires that the language of the original work must be largely abandoned to that of the language into which it is being translated. However, this translator has taken the decision to allow certain few elements of the Spanish in which the work was written to remain, to be imported into the English version, with the end of providing the feeling and sentiment inherent to the author's expression, to wit, beyond the footnotes found throughout the work, the following explanations are provided:

Firstly: The diminutive suffix "-ito, -ita," which at times requires the shifting, omition, or addition of preceding letters necessary to phonetics.

Examples: The name Manuel becomes Manuelito, Carla becomes Carlita, while Paco (short for Francisco) becomes Paquito. There are various permutations, but this is the basic orthography.

As the suffix simply means little, then Pablito means "little Pablo," or "poco" (which means small/little) when changed to "poquito" would be translated as "very small" or "un poquito" could mean "a little bit" depending on the context.

In this work practically all the diminutives are applied to people's names, and in this context they are terms of endearment, i.e. when one attaches an "-ito," or "-ita," on someone's name, it expresses love, affection, familiarity or affinity. The author makes copious use of this device throughout the work.

Futhermore, the author employs a personal adaptation of the diminutive when referring to his father or mother: "Papá" would normally become "Papito," and "Mamá" "Mamita." Here the author prefers his invention: "Papaíto" (pronounced like Popeye ending with -tō) and "Mamaíta."

Secondly: The author affectionately uses the possessive adjective "mi" (my) when referring to family members – "Mi papá" or "Mi Ernesto." This form remains in the translation, using "mi" (pronounced "me") instead of "my."

Finally, certain accents necessary to proper Spanish pronunciation remain.

PART ONE

My grandma Pola attends eleven o'clock mass

The happiest day of the week for my grandmother Pola was Sunday, and the most awaited hour, eleven o'clock in the morning. Every Sunday, my grandmother went to eleven o'clock mass in the Cathedral Church of Cajamarca. A white *mantilla*[1] crowned her gray hair. Two black combs held the beautiful garment that fell over her whitish hair and gently slid down her back. This long and immaculate mantilla made her stand out from the other attendees: Miss Filomena and Miss Esther Rodriguez, who, dressed in rigorous mourning attire, escorted Grandma Pola as they descended Cajamarca Street, crossed *Jirón*[2] Comercio and walked a little further until they reached the gates of the majestic baroque cathedral at 10:45 in the morning. That Sunday we formed the entourage consisting of Gonzalo; my father, grandmother's eldest son, always dressed in one of his continual gray suits, Francisco; Uncle Paquito, dressed in a silver Sunday suit, blue tie and patent leather shoes, Delishita; in a representative black suit imitating her mother, a small pearl-colored scarf, white stockings that covered her ankles and well-polished black slippers that never got dirty beyond the edge of the soles, Perpetuita; always radiant, who only took Delishita's arm on Sundays, on other days she held her hand; and me, young Paquito. Julish did not accompany us because he was always traveling.

---

1 Veil

2 Lane or street

My grandmother would cry when the phone rang and Julish would be on the phone from some corner of the world. My brother Mánuel, the first of my siblings, once, when alarmed by my grandmother's tears, told me that she was crying for joy and not out of sadness, when she heard her son's voice.

Behind me was my mother Mechita, accompanied each year by one more child. At that time there were five of us children surrounding my mother, Mánuel, the oldest; Érnesto; me, Paquito; *mi*[3] Coque, and mi Pepe. That's how I called them: mi Mánuel, with the accent on the first syllable, on the letter a; mi Érnesto, with the accent on the first e; mi Coque and mi Pepe. That is how they also called each other. My brothers called me mi Paquish, other people called me *el niño Paquito.*

And what's the story? I'm sure you're wondering.

The story is that the mischievous Paquito, who was four years old at the time, and who was once again bored with mass, with nothing else to distract him, he lay down on the church pew, laying his head on his Grandmother Pola's lap, making her believe he was asleep, all in order to put his plan into action. As he had learned the Latin mass by rote – which was the language in which masses were celebrated at that time – as surely as his brothers, other children and townspeople had done by listening to it so much; el niño Paquito came up with the idea of anticipating the words of Father Mundaca (that was the priest's last name) as a way of getting out of there as soon as possible.

On previous occasions, after the "*dominus vobiscum.*" Paquito would intervene, before the parishioners, and answer: "*Et cum spiritu tuo.*" The priest had barely opened his mouth, before Paquito would say: "*Orate frates.*" He did it so quickly that the attendants no longer answered the priest, but

---

3 My

rather Paquito: "*Dignum et justum es.*" But that morning, el niño Paquito said: "*Per omnia saecula saeculorum*," and the parishioners answered: "*Amen.*" At that moment, he realized that Grandma Pola had fallen asleep, and took advantage of the situation to continue. Then, in a very loud singing voice as he stood up to end the mass, he said; "*In nomine Patris et Filii et Spiritus Sancti*," and pulled his grandmother by the arm, responding; "*Amen.*" Finally, in order to conclude the ceremony, Paquito added, "*Dominus vosbiscum.* In your belly *te peñiscum*," and he yanked once more on his grandmother's arm.

Right there and then the mass ended, grandma woke up, amid the sermon and doctrine. Sweet little Grandma Pola stood up, believing that the mass was really over. Followed by her entourage, she left the church, and behind that retinue, a huge crowd followed. The priest Mundaca, perplexed by such a situation, as a means for an intelligent reply only managed to chant in Latin: "*In ipso vita erat, et vita erat lux hominum et lux in tenebris lucet.*"

Thus concluded mass in the Cathedral of Cajamarca.

Never has such a short Catholic mass been witnessed in all the world, least of all those that were given in Latin.

Behind the pool, crowned by the blue sky, stands the beautiful baroque cathedral of the city of Cajamarca. My grandmother, Mrs. Pola Delia Cacho Sousa, used to go there on Sundays to listen to the 11:00 a.m. mass. Note the absence of towers in the church (Photo by the Regional Government)

Grumpy, the white cat

Each and every month of October my grandmother Pola changed her black dress for a purple one, in supplication of devotion to *el Señor de los Milagros*,[4] patron saint of the city of Lima.

Paquito never understood how a lady from Cajamarca, naturally devoted to *Nuestra Señora de los Dolores*[5] (for whom she was even given a beautiful black mantle, embroidered in silver and gold threads, which she still wears during Holy Week), could have "strayed" towards such a fervent devotion to a patron saint from out of town. But this is of little importance, since it is known that, as far as Paquito is concerned, *el Señor de los Milagros* is of little significance. Perhaps he only said that out of pure jealousy or suspicion, not understanding that there could be someone more important and wonderful than *Nuestra Señora de los Dolores.*

In the month of October, or rather, every month of October, my *Abuelita* Pola not only changed the black dress and the white scarf for the purple "habit" and the white cord around her waist. She also exchanged the Cajamarca *rosquitas*[6] and the buttery cheese (so delicious!) for the candy sprinkles and strange nougat of *Doña Pepa*,[7] which her brother Manuelito regularly and without fail sent her from the city of Lima every year in the month of October.

At the foot of the bed, in the bedroom, my grandmother Pola had an oak table covered with a white tablecloth, which was exchanged for a purple one in October. On that table she

---

4 The Lord of Miracles

5 Our Lady of Suffering

6 Little cookies

7 Name given to the little cakes related to this character which is the Peruvian equivalent to Aunt Jemima

would have her five o'clock *lonche*.[8] I think my grandmother only left the bedroom to go to mass. On the table sat the cutlery and a bottle of aniseed liqueur to reduce the rigors resulting from the always abundant food.

My grandmother was a very good eater, as almost all grandmothers are. Under the table was her white cat. The white cat was always there; he was white from head to toe, including his claws, eyebrows, eyelashes, and tail. White from the haunches to the tip of the tail. He should have been named Snow or Polar like my granddaughter Francisca's dog, but in this story we will call him Grumpy.

The white cat would only consent to my grandmother's affection. He was coarse, grumpy, he would raise his haunches if you so much as looked at him and if you got even a little bit closer, Grumpy, the white cat, would emit a repetitive and intimidating "quifff." These sounds were snorts like those of an angry bull, but in a high-pitched tone, it was "quifff," "quifff," dangerous.

The cat was always under the table, for there my grandmother would fawn on him, cajole him by giving him bits of cheese during any month other than October, which was when she gave him pieces of nougat of Doña Pepa, which put the nasty white cat in an even worse mood.

Paquito, every time he entered his grandmother's bedroom, annoyed the cat. Needless to say, the cat and Paquito were bitter enemies, a glance from Paquito and a step forward would provoke a series of snorts and a pronounced hunched back from the cat.

Every time Paquito pushed him with his foot, the cat would go: "quifff" and more "quifff." But this time, the cat was so awnry that when Paquito gave him a single flick on his nose

8 A late afternoon supper

with his finger, he jumped on Paquito's face and scratched the tip of his nose. The wound took seven days to mend, after which Paquito swore to take revenge.

Days later, Paquito – with a well-contrived plan – confronted the cat again: he gave him another, harder flick on the nose. The cat, of course, growled at him but the provocation still was not enough to make the cat fall into the trap. Paquito flicked his nose again. This time, the white cat raised its haunches and jumped towards Paquito's face with its claws out. At that instant, Paquito was ready, he squatted down and with both hands caught the cat and put him in a small cotton-cloth sack. He swung it around in the air until it got dizzy, and then released him.

Grandma, who had no idea what had happened, observed the cat to be quite dizzy, staggering, and then Paquito raised his accusation and told her: "Grandma, the cat is drunk: he has gotten into the aniseed liquor." Needless to say, from that day on, the cat was forbidden from entering grandma's room ever again.

A basket of provincial eggs

My father Gonzalito was a sailor, he had loved this profession ever since he was a child because of his visits to the sea. He often went to the port of Pacasmayo, which was reached by train from Chilete, a warm and hospitable little town. From Cajamarca to Chilete one went by bus, by car or by cab, because the distance was great: more than six hours away.

For her part, my mother Delish, many years later – when the train no longer existed and only a couple of rails embedded in the ground of the main square had been left as a last trace – spent a vacation in Chilete with Alicia, my mother Perpetua, and my brother Rafi. My mother was just looking for a bit of warmth, as she was feeling quite cold.

In Chilete, the days passed uneventfully, there were few things to do: sleep, have breakfast with coffee, warm bread, and from time to time, a taste of fried fish; go for a visit to the river in the mornings to dip your feet, and then return for a lunch of chicken soup, beans boiled in their skins, and mashed potatoes with lentils.

However, the exception to that routine was an invitation my mother received for lunch at the small farm of her good friend Blanquita Rabanal. There they served crab soup, which mi Rafi refused to eat, but not before – at only three or four years of age – he dared to make a beautiful and articulate speech: "Thank you very much, dear and hospitable friends, thank you for the invitation, but I am not going to eat this spider soup," he said, and then the laughter of the diners was not long in coming. He was not discouraged by the guffaws, rather, he quite smugly went out for a little stroll, leaving his plate as it was served, the attendees were astonished by his easy-going personality.

Telling you all about Chilete is relevant, because my Uncle Paquito went there on his way to Lima when he was 14 years old while travelling to the capital to visit his brother Gonzalito, who at that time was already a cadet at the Peruvian Naval Academy.

Uncle Paquito's trip started in Cajamarca on an old public transportation bus, within six hours he had then arrived in Chilete, from there he went by train on a five-hour trip to Pacasmayo. Once in Pacasmayo he went to Trujillo, where he arrived after seven hours. After sleeping at the home of an aunt and uncle named Pinillas, he then boarded another, more modern, bus system called Tahuantinsuyo very early the next morning, embarking on the final leg of the trip to the city of Lima, which took an additional twelve hours.

The naval school cadet, mi Papaíto, that's how we called him, Papaíto, not papito nor Papá, we simply called him Papaíto. He was born in Huaraz, but grew up in Cajamarca and considered himself a native of Cajamarca. He reached the rank of captain, although he preferred to say first lieutenant to distinguish himself as a sailor: he always made it clear to us that he was a navy man, not a merchant marine: being a navy man was a source of pride for him.

His classmates from the Naval School were always very dear to him, we called them uncles. We used to call the man who later became Admiral Alberto Jiménez de Lucio, Uncle Becho, and we did the same with our uncles: Javier Pinillos Taboada, Tomasito Pizarro, Kiko Mazuré, Jorge Arnillas de la Cotera, Pachi Paredes Arana, Carlos Jesús Boza, whom Papaíto called Cárlos Jesús, Lucho Guerioni, Uncle Jorge "Negro" Parra del Riego and many others.

When Papaíto entered the Naval Academy he was immediately assimilated as one more young member of Lima's high society. His provincial *Cajamarquino* speech did not keep him from rubbing shoulders with the outstanding sailors of that time. That a *serrano*[9] from Cajamarca was so white, freckled and red haired, rather provoked admiration among his companions; they affectionately called him *Serrano Coloradito*,[10] but that nickname did not sound like that as you have read it, in truth they pronounced it in this way: "Seshrano Coloradito," making the double "r" sound like "ershe," making fun of the serrano way of speaking.

Gonzalito stood out for his math skills and discipline. Papaíto struggled to be just one more, a *Limeño*,[11] just another cadet at the Peruvian Naval Academy, so as not to be the target of his classmates' mockery. Some problems would arise on weekends when he went to a party where there were girls with whom he had to talk; he was never good at dancing, and worse still, because his ear was attuned to the *huayno*,[12] and not to rock and roll. In the afternoons at my Papá Manuelito's house, in front of the full-length mirror that my Aunt Teresita had behind her bedroom door, he practiced the dance moves, the rock, that his cousins Shurita and Delita taught him.

As from the first day at the Naval School, his slow and song-like speech that his *Cajamarquino*[13] roots bestowed upon him, as well as his pronunciation of the letter "rr," worse situations befell him. He made efforts to pronounce the blessed letter by vibrating the tip of his tongue, not as he currently did by dragging the "r" with the sound of "sh," which as aforementioned, is common in the speech of serranos. His companions tried to catch him at any "eshe" instead of a trilled "erre" sound, in

9 *Serrano/serrana* - someone native to the sierra - mountains

10 Colorado refers to someone or something having a red or blond hue

11 Native to Lima

12 A style of folk music and dance common to the sierra

13 From or pertaining to Cajamarca

order to provoke their laughter. He considered himself to be provincial and serrano, with more than a little pride, and more vainly Cajamarquino, but he sincerely would have preferred not to be subjected to those situations.

Now, as a first year cadet, and after only a few months of adaptation, in the month of July, the schoolgirls who were on vacation, thanks to the days of patriotic celebration in Peru, would go to the port to see the cadets who, on Saturday mornings dressed in impeccable dress uniform. The handsome uniformed men would emerge from the academy's door, or disembark from some ship on which, presumptuously, they were preparing themselves in case of naval war.

The cadets were getting off the ship, elegant, haughty, smiling: they looked beautiful. But even more beautiful were the schoolgirls, the slightly older girls, their relatives, and the few friends who were waiting at the foot of the esplanade. The sailors descended from the ships by cat ladders made of ropes and wooden slats, while the cadets and officers were assisted by the combat ladders, made of iron and chains which, at the top end, were attached to the edge of the ship on the structure of the deck with two hooks, while at the bottom, two plates or flat legs held fast to the hull of the ship from the weight of the bodies that descended or ascended.

Only the commander of the ship or the high authorities who visited the combat ships could use the "royal staircase" which was wider and was made like a tower. The royal staircase allowed one to get on and off the ships with comfort and great majesty, it was usually kept shiny and painted in white.

On the third Saturday of July, cadet Gonzalo, mi Papaíto, was waiting for his brother Paquito's visit. Before getting off the ship, his shipmates, naval cadets, proposed to impress Uncle Paquito, who at that time was a very handsome young man of about fourteen years old.

On that impressive sunny day, nearing the national holiday, many girls and relatives of the naval students would be going to the esplanade to see the first year cadets on their first excursion on the flagship of the National Navy. The cadets, Gonzalo's companions, and he as well – quite enthused –, hatched a plan to wait until the officers had left and were sufficiently far off to prevent their ability to see the ship. Thus they plotted to reposition the royal staircase, which they were forbidden to use, and they proposed that Gonzalito should disembark by this means, with them following right behind. In this way, not only would Uncle Paquito be greatly impressed, but also the dozens of young women who wanted to see, not their brothers and cousins, but the cadets of the Naval Academy.

It was the perfect plan, at nine-fifteen in the morning, at the top of the ship, Gonzalito was seen descending, followed by a court of young men, each one svelte in his white uniform; the four sailors, all in cahoots, dragged the royal staircase into place and, to the sound of the navy band intoning the flag march, Gonzalito and his entourage descended from the flagship bearing the name of the Great Admiral of the seas, *Miguel Grau Seminario*. Gonzalito, nervous but firm, as he descended from the highest to the last step of the royal staircase, almost stumbling, looked up and saw my Uncle Paquito and, behind him, his Papá Manuelito and my Aunt Teresita. The presence of both the aunt and uncle made the occasion even more special, dozens of young women were attentive, and the companions proud.

The surprise would have something extra: when Gonzalito reached the shore, the cadets would take off their caps and give three cheers in his honor.

Once the cadets raised their caps, the one who caused a stupor was Uncle Paquito, who made his way to the group and, approaching his brother, stood in front of him and the cadets, holding a little basket that he had brought very carefully with both arms outstretched in front of him. In a loud voice with his charming Cajamarca accent that everyone could hear said: "Little brother, I brought you some eggs in this little basket, be careful they don't '*shrompan*'."[14] As expected, the surprise, the laughter and the mockery of his companions were not long in coming. The latter, the mockery, was repeated many years later, remembering this story painting Gonzalito as a provincial "seshrrano" with eggs in a little basket.

The first flagship of the Peruvian Navy, BAP Almirante Miguel Grau, in the 1930s, 1940s and 1950s, still in service (photo taken from the internet)

14 The imperative of "break" (romper) pronounced with the serrano "sh"

My grandfather Gonzalos' tips

My Grandfather Gonzalo, mi Papaíto's father, lived in Chiclayo. He was a man of medium height and gray hair. His handsome face was adorned with circular glasses giving him an intellectual air, and the tenderness with which he spoke conquered everyone, especially women. Always lucid, one could say that he was adorned with congeniality and he exploited it.

A confusing sensation provoked my awareness that I was going to see my grandfather. His divorce with my grandmother wreaked havoc on the family: my grandmother never spoke about him, my mother Delishita suffered so much grief and resentment – she even hated the law profession and forbade me to study to become a lawyer, as my grandfather had done. It was natural that mi Delishita felt sorrow when remembering or thinking about my grandfather, her estranged father. That sorrow within some small part of her soul, caused by a lost marriage and a distant father, wouldn't allow her be happy. The restless love she felt for her father, my Grandfather Gonzalo, became evident simply by talking about him or mentioning him.

I remember traveling to Chiclayo to visit my grandfather maybe once or twice, but no more than three times. The drive to Pimentel was beautiful, but it wasn't the most beautiful thing on those trips. The window displays on Main Street, the toy wagons displayed in the windows or just looking at the women's shoes displayed in the stores delighted my mother Delishita and me; she knew I wanted some new shoes, I didn't know what I wanted, but I loved walking around and looking in the windows and at the lights. I loved new shoes, but I preferred riding boots. There were no riding boots on the street in Chiclayo, there were lights, lots of lights, toy wagons and little soldiers, they were beautiful, I didn't want to have them, I just wanted to see them and know that they were there.

My mother Delish, a primary school teacher (sorry, I'm mistaken, director of a little school, the 125th in Cajamarca), did not have much in the way of economic resources, but she had a huge heart. She was very small, we have already mentioned that she was called *Pasita*.[15] Delishita had an immense spirit and an especially immense love for me, greater than that which she felt for all of my siblings, until my brother Rafito was born, whom she loved as much as she did me. If you did not understand this last point, allow me to repeat: she loved him so much, so great was her love for her son Rafito, that she loved him as much as she loved me.

My grandfather used to take us to the beach at Pimentel, we would go for a walk to see the ocean. I didn't go into the water, I didn't like to bathe in it, I didn't know how to swim. I liked riding horses. I also liked to jump, I liked to jump in an unusual way. I remember dreaming so many times that I jumped so much, so high and so very far. I remember having these dreams, dreams of long jumps, almost like flying, on many, many occasions. I remember having them repeatedly until I was well into my adolescence.

My grandfather would talk quietly with my Delishita. They always talked about the same thing, about how great the sea is, about the delicious Cajamarquino *semitas* and the sweetened *rosquitas*[16] sold by the dear nuns cloistered in the convent of La Concepción. They talked about other things, about food, there were no conceptual themes, no talk of feelings or emotions, except for the occasional wounded seagull fallen from the skies, which I never saw happen.

---

15 Little Raisin

16 Semita – a type of sweet roll, Rosquita – a little cookie

The walk and lunch in Pimentel took place on the first day of the visit; the second day we would go to the town of Santa Rosa, also by the seashore; on the third day, as always on Sunday after mass, we had lunch at the city's social club. The walks were itineraries of conversation and lunch, the latter being the most important thing. Visits to Chiclayo were pure protocol: "a daughter should visit her father, a good father should walk with his daughter." I had to accompany my mother.

Delishita and I ate very little. My grandfather always started lunch with a glass of *pisco*[17] sour and then some sea bass ceviche. When we went to Pimentel, the second course, after the usual rock sea bass with lime and *aji*,[18] was a huge tray of rice with duck that the three of us would share. My grandfather ate all of the ceviche, my mother Delish did not eat ceviche and I had never eaten any fish, least of all raw fish. When we used to go to the Santa Rosa beach resort, the meal was goat *Chiclayana*[19] style with *loche* (loche is a small pre–Columbian squash native to the area).

Lunches with my grandfather always had two happy endings: vanilla ice cream and tips for the waiters. My mother Delish invariably had two scoops of ice cream, I only had one (I needed to stay light to be able to jump). My mother Delish complemented the ice cream with a dab of sugar which she would pop into her mouth all at once; she loved sugar, she preferred sweet to salty, and she taught me that. A cup of ice cream made me happy, but the tip my grandfather left after lunch made me even happier. My grandfather always left a few coins for the waiters and some for me. In Pimentel and Santa

17 A grape liquor native to Peru

18 Chili

19 From or pertaining to Chiclayo

Rosa, the waiters' tips consisted of three or four half *sol*[20] coins. Mine consisted of much more, they were with smaller coins, but many more, sometimes up to ten or twelve one-*peseta* coins (twenty cents) or *real* (ten cents). It was evident that my grandfather loved me much more than the waiters of Pimentel and Santa Rosa.

If you think this story is over, you are wrong. The last day of the visit with my grandfather in Chiclayo always ended with a lunch at the most distinguished club in town. The tables had tablecloths, three knives, a spoon, two teaspoons, a white cloth napkin tucked into a silver ring, a plump maître d' dressed in a black suit and tie, and five or six waiters dressed elegantly in black pants and white jackets. In this tranquil place, as a second course after the usual sea bass ceviche, without having to ask, just with a look from my grandfather, the waiters hurriedly and attentively served us thickened ground corn (like mashed potatoes) with beef brisket and yellow rice. For me, this dish was the most delicious because, as a good Cajamarquino serrano, I liked corn more than duck or goat. Chiclayano cuisine is among the best in Peru. For my mother Delish the best thing was a dab of sugar at the end of lunch. The sugar tasted much better to my mother if she had drunk one or two pisco sours beforehand, like this time, along with her father.

The happy ending in the main dining room of the social club turned out wonderfully. On the previous trip, my grandfather tipped the waiters and there, in that more distinguished place, the tip was bigger than in Pimentel or Santa Rosa. My tip on the previous trip was also much higher at the social club than at the beaches of Chiclayo.

20 Sol means sun, and is also the currency in Peru

This last time, at the end of lunch, the tip came. As it was the last day of the visit, there were also two pisco sours apiece, two for my grandfather and two for mi Delish; however, as it was the day of farewells, the pisco sours were "Cathedral" sized. That night we would have to go to the Diaz & Diaz transportation company to take the bus back to Cajamarca. The results of the huge drinks were very cheerful: "I love you, my dear daughter," "I love you too, *mí papito*," were the most frequent phrases in the conversation. The moment of tipping was fantastic: my grandfather left three bills of ten soles on the table. The bills made a single pile, so the maître d', the head waiter, considered it to be his regular tip. Since my grandfather had not reached into his pocket again, I assumed that at least two of the bills would be for me. Judging from what I will now describe, so did my mother Delish. As to better explain the situation, I should comment that every time my grandfather left me the little tip of coins, and I picked them up, the joy in my mother's little eyes was greater than what I felt. Her two shining lights twinkled in unison with her huge smile.

I watched the tipping scene at the social club as if it were in slow motion: the maître d', after looking happily sideways at the two waiters behind him, took the three bills with his long, fat arm. My little hand only managed to graze the hand of the obese giant, my mother Delish jumped over the chair and pounced on the maître d', who already had his back to us. My mother could not grab the gorilla's hand, but she did reach his belt, the maître d' took three or four steps and dragged my mother, who wouldn't let go of the scallywag; three more steps and my mother still would not let go, my grandfather's eyes were wide with fright; Delish who prevented the maître d' from moving forward, the obese man who insisted on walking, me who grabbed my mother from behind, my grandfather holding me from behind, the greedy head waiter was impossible to stop. We looked like a train of bodies pulled by a colossal locomotive. The customers sitting at other tables stood up. After a few moments of struggling, the train became longer because the maître d' lost his pants, they fell down to the level of his thighs, even so, the train continued its march towards the swinging door of the kitchen.

Happily, good sense reigned: my grandfather raised his arms and let go of the train, and this prudent action ended with us all scattered across the floor. My grandfather Gonzalo, with his arms raised, sitting on the kitchen floor, only managed to say: "The Lord is my shepherd, I shall not want." This he said as a sign of resignation and supplication to the All Mighty.

Grandfather Gonzalo Sáenz Zamarán, Papaíto and Manuel in the Fifties

The invisible little horse

As far as I can remember, there were more than two occasions when I stayed with my Papá Manuelito (godfather at my baptism and my grandmother Pola's older brother), at 737 Santa Cruz Street, in the Jesús María district of Lima.

The times I remember the most are these: the first, when I was only four years old and was about to turn five, which would have been in July 1958, and the second, some weeks after the death of my Grandmother Pola in December 1965, when I was about twelve years old.

That second time was around the month of March 1966, after a long stay in La Joyita, the beautiful hacienda home and land of my Uncle Carlitos and his wife Aunt Mary, on the outskirts of Chiclayo. The death of my Grandmother Pola left my mother Delish's spirit devastated. Grief accompanied her everywhere, during the day she sobbed from time to time, at night she woke up in a sea of tears because the Ecuanil, a tranquilizer pill for her nerves, did not produce the desired effect. The infinite kindness of Uncle Carlitos and Aunt Mary welcomed us to La Joyita and weeks later, we were generously invited to Papá Manuelito's home.

On the second trip during the summer of 1966, my Papá Manuelito patiently and affectionately waited for us at the Tahuantinsuyo transport agency in the center of the city of Lima (we were arriving from Pacasmayo where we stayed one night at the Hotel Ferrocarril). That would have been five o'clock in the afternoon, no later than six; the visit included several of us: mi Delishita, mi Mamita Perpetua, Alicia, my brother Rafito, who was about four years old, and me. The imperturbable, gray uniformed driver greeted us, after which I never heard another word from his mouth, neither that afternoon nor in the following days of our stay; he was their same driver over many years, the same one who picked us up the first time more than five or six years previous (although in that first immoderate visit Rafito was not there, it must have been seven years before). The driver of the luxurious black car simply kept his eyes on the road and drove with a smoothness that I had never enjoyed before. The turns around the corners were taken with a wide trajectory, but without invading the opposing lane. There were no speed bumps, rather slow stops deliberately taken at every block. The car and driver were undoubtedly accustomed to taking Papá Manuelito and Tía Teresita on morning rides and, in the evenings, to elegant dinners such as those at the governmental palace in previous years. It was easy to understand how, while serving a couple of glasses of champagne, not a drop would be spilled on such sublime trips.

The conversations between Delishita and my Papá Manuelito always went very smoothly. They treated each other as "*hijita*"[21] and "Papá Manuelito," as they called each other while they talked about the noble profession of teaching, when not about childhood memories or the prayers of my Grandmother Pola. Papá Manuelito was very affectionate with me, he called me "Paquito" or "my godson." His masculine face had an air of solvency and security, his unhurried and affectionate speech was engaging; that must have been how he was as a politician: he enthused people and stole their hearts. My Aunt Teresita was no less kind or engaging in her gentleness or presence: she was a tall woman and her bearing and elegance were impressive. With a single glance she commanded respect while at the same time transmitting peace; her voice was serene, poised, never a word too many. Perhaps her manners were different from those of my Papá Manuelito, but the harmony they had together was calming

21 Little daughter

and comforting, and this was what my mother Delia needed most. This harmony which I had admired on the second trip, was the same I felt during the first one, of which I have great memories in spite of my young age at the time.

The first trip took place, if someone with a better memory cannot contradict me, in the summer of 1958. I am sure of the date because I wore a bright, shiny aluminum-colored, medium-sized gift for men on my left wrist. It had a medium-sized black strap and told the time. My Papá Manuelito gave it to me on his previous trip to Cajamarca, he had given it to me right on my birthday, the seventeenth day of the seventh month of 1957, and I remember it very well because he himself set the hands to seven past seven. This gift differed from a similar instrument, a beautiful five-star Longines women's watch that my mother Delish proudly wore on her tiny, freckled right wrist; she wore it there so as to avoid provoking the delinquents while she drove her Mercury automobile, that immense car which, given her small stature, required the use of a fat white cotton cushion and a wooden block attached to the clutch pedal in order for her to drive it.

As already mentioned, on the first trip (the one Rafito did not go on) there were four of us visitors at my Papá Manuelito's and Aunt Teresita's house: Delishita, Mamita Perpetua, Alicia, and me. Every afternoon I would watch television in my great aunt and uncle's room. Papá Manuelito would go to the Senate to work. My Aunt Teresita and I used to watch Rin-Tin-Tin and also the horse Furia; this last name I gave years later to a black colt I had in Polloc. My Aunt Teresita had a very tall bed, I don't know if she was ill or if she needed a bed of such size because she was big, bigger than me, my mother, Alicia, and Mamita Perpetua. I considered my Aunt Teresita bigger than my Papá Manuelito. I'm not sure whether the latter was true, or if it was just her majesty that gave me that impression.

My aunt's largesse not only endured my long hours invading her privacy, it also endured my constant running to the television set to change the channel. There were only three channels. Panamericana Television on channel thirteen and Radio America Television on channel four were both my and my aunt Teresita's favorites. The government's channel seven was my Papá Manuelito's favorite, but he only watched it at night, so he didn't interrupt my Aunt Teresita and me with Rin-Tin-Tin, Furia, and some soap operas with people kissing each other.

Patience accompanied the largesse of my Aunt Teresita. From time to time, her white hand caressed my little well combed head with its perfect part combed on the left side. This happened during television time, which was wonderful. While my mother and her two companions prayed in a little room on the second floor or sunbathed in the Sevillian patio, I watched television with my Aunt Teresita. There was no television in Cajamarca, so watching it was a delight for me.

The noise I made in the house must have been very annoying, but my Aunt Teresita found it charming, at least that's what I thought. I would jump out of the second floor windows onto the first floor roof. Riding my invisible horse, I would follow a route that started in the kitchen on the second floor and ended in the hall on the second floor, if not in the very center of my Aunt Teresita's room.

The route of my fantastic horse, which trotted, galloped and then rapidly ran, started in the morning after breakfast. It would start from the kitchen after the rider said thanks for the always warm buttered rolls, continued climbing the main staircase to the second floor, crossing the space between the bedroom doors, entered the bedroom at the back assigned to us visitors; all this imitating the gentle gait of the finest Peruvian horses; I crossed the room, greeting my Mamita Perpetua and Alicia with a gesture of taking off a hat and showing off before the qualifying jury, then with a majestic jump I climbed through the window that overlooked the roof of the second floor; once there we galloped across the entire white and undulating roof that covered the house, continued with a leap to a lower roof and instantly, with another jump; entered through the low window of an empty room.

On the second floor my fictitious horse ran towards the door exiting the unoccupied room, entering the small door towards the garage at full speed, and circled the parked black car twice. The driver, half frightened, half angry, would violently shew the horse with a flannel rag he used to keep "*la sala que sale*"[22] clean (that's how my Papá Manuelito called his car, he called it "la sala que sale" meaning that it should always be kept spotless), and then the fantastic steed would arrive through the small door towards the entrance near the hallways of the wonderful residence; the rider would give a wink to the telephone that was waiting for him on a beautiful marble table. The horse, always in swift flight, would turn towards the main staircase and, taking it with strides that covered two or three steps at a time, would arrive again at the hallway on the second floor to begin a new lap.

Television after lunch in the afternoons, lunches were very uplifting at my Papá Manuelito and Aunt Teresita's house. The conversation was different than at the house in Cajamarca, the food was not the same; in Cajamarca there was *chochoca*[23] soup, if it not semolina, once in while there was chicken soup with just a little chicken because three hens were never enough for so many inhabitants. At my godfather's house they had salads and boiled vegetables, the first ones were delicious if you added a dressing of lemon, salt and half a teaspoon of something unknown to me that had a dark yellow color, which now I

22 The room that travels

23 Cornmeal

understand was mustard and that my Aunt Teresita prepared personally; the parboiled vegetables consisting of beans, carrots, and peas did not taste good to me, especially because they did not include boiled serrano potatoes, no mattter if they did come with some little worms. The second course in Cajamarca always came with rice "*atamalado*,"[24] a terrible rice prepared by mi Juanachita, my grandmother's cook. She never could prepare rice well. Juanachita was a lousy cook, but she was the stew chef whom my grandmother loved with great tenderness.

At Aunt Teresita's house, cracked rice was served accompanied with some stew or fried meat, the same as in Cajamarca. Sometimes there was fish (in Cajamarca there was no fish). Every year the protesters took to the streets demanding that the authorities build a meat packing plant. It was never built while I was living in Cajamarca, which was until 1970. I don't remember if dessert was served. My mother loved desserts. I'm sure she was served jello or ice cream. I liked ice cream, but my horse ate my Aunt Teresita's very select fruits in order to stay healthy.

The uplifting lunches were more for the soul and intellect than for the body. Tender expressions and constant affection was felt in every sentence, in every conversation, the most used word was the possessive "mi" to refer to any member of the family, the diminutives –ito, –ita, –shito, –shita were repeated during all the lunches. These beautiful ceremonies began with giving thanks to the Lord for the food, the prayer given by any of the three adults. The table was presided over by my Papá Manuelito from the far side of the large dining room. There were only four of us at the big table, the two hosts, my mother and me; my mother at the far edge of the table on the left side, to the right of Papá Manuelito, my aunt Teresita at the other end and me to her right, forming a right angle. It could be said that the table had two

24 Rice, cooked with beans, potatoes, onions and garlic

corners: to the north, the uncle and the niece and to the south, diagonally, the aunt and the little grandson. The most edifying part began after constructive comments about each of the relatives, then national economic, social and educational affairs. The topics were treated with the utmost frankness. That was the first time I heard about a certain Keynes, I understood the difference between sowing and reaping, I also understood the meaning of the word honor, I understood why someone could fight a duel.

The saddest lunch was the one in which Aunt Teresita, smiling, asked me if my horse could stop running around so much, she told me that it did it endlessly as if it were the second hand of a clock. I sensed that the running might be bothering her, although it did not show on her saintly face. I got the message, and from that day on, until our departure, my little invisible horse went around counterclockwise, going out through the garage, up through the empty bedroom window into the bedroom and finally down the stairs.

Papá Manuelito and Aunt Teresita in 1970

The little black telephone

On that same trip to Lima in the summer of 1958, in the house of my Papá Manuelito and Aunt Teresita, after about a two week stay, during one of the peaceful lunch hours, I was happy to hear some news: my Papá Manuelito announced that the next day my uncles Luchito, Carlitos, and Jaimito, his beloved sons, would come for breakfast; he said they would have to deal with adult issues and that I should please put the horse away that morning and go for a walk. This would be a reason to visit my Aunt Viruchita during lunch, in her big second story house on Bolognesi Plaza. This news also made me happy because it was certain that the first course at Aunt Viruchita's house would be stuffed avocado. Aunt Viruchita's three or four cooks always served us a very large stuffed avocado. I loved the avocado and the stuffing of sliced potatoes with a few carrots, and no beets, if it came with homemade mayonnaise. Aunt Viruchita hosted many people at her house, all former employees of one of her seven haciendas, or "Cachito" relatives (that's how we called relatives with the last name Cacho, descendants of some branch of Uncle Nemesio Cacho, an individual of exacerbated sexuality, who left descendants all over the place). His niece Yolita was the favorite; Papaíto teased her be saying: *Yola Cacho*,[25] alluding to a not so humorous sexual connotation. Although lunches at the homes of either of our Cacho or Cacho-Sousa relatives were always served a little late (except at Papá Manuelito's house), they were never as late as at my Aunt Tulita Rodriquez's house in Cajamarca, who served lunch after four in the afternoon, when the guests,

25 A play on words: separating the name Yola into Yo "I" and la "her," plus the surname Cacho (cachar) is also slang for "fornicate" – *Yo la cacho*

usually my mother Delish and I, were nearly faint with hunger. I was very happy to know that my Aunt Elenita, who lived with my Aunt Viruchita, would give me a large chocolate with hazelnuts after dinner and before saying goodbye. The chocolate was wrapped on the outside in a luxurious and shiny red paper that showed a picture of chocolate and hazelnuts. On that same wrapper and in white letters was a phrase that read: "Delicious Swiss milk chocolate and hazelnuts."

I greedily tore the red wrapper, hurriedly tore the very thin platinum paper and found inside the delicious Swiss milk chocolate, which was only sold in Lima (there was none Cajamarca) and was always delicious, even more so when it was only for me. Aunt Elenita's chocolates were more than twenty centimeters long by five centimeters wide, a quarter of an inch thick, they stuck to my fingers in the Lima heat, melted in my mouth and from time to time gave me a hazelnut that exploded crunchily between my molars. Needless to say, my little fingers smeared in chocolate, when sucked one by one, also tasted delicious.

Breakfast that Sunday was served in the main dining room at Santa Cruz 737, at Papá Manuelito's house. It was a lively time. My three uncles ate a lot, Uncle Luchito a little more, who at times took portions of *chicharron*[26] with his fingers and, before making them into a sandwich, would bite off half of each portion; Uncle Carlitos was the liveliest one in the conversation and drank up to three cups of coffee; Uncle Jaimito appeared measured and elegant. I watched as the tamales and fried pork disappeared like magic, happily I reached for a half of a roll of bread with chicharron, which was enough for me because two or three delicious spongy rolls with butter, satisfied me; a cup of milk with Milo that had been bought for me

26 Pork rinds

gave me the energy to ride my horse, but I remembered that there would be no riding that day.

Having nothing to do until noon, I devoted myself to using the telephone, the one that was on the little marble table near the kitchen door, and to which I gave a wink every time I passed by on my little invisible horse. It was black and had a circle that spun as I dialed the numbers until a small crescent-moon stop that prevented it from any further spinning with my finger. The magic circle would stop at each number dialed when it reached the crescent stop. I knew the telephone numbers of my Aunt Viruchita, my Grandfather Ernesto, my Uncle Alberto and also, of course, my Papá Manuelito by heart. As the polite child that I was, I made several calls to say hello to my grandfather, my aunts and my Uncle Alberto. My grandfather Ernesto's number was 223-6692, I called him, greeted him and he told me that they were waiting for us to have lunch and to go to the beach on the Saturday of the following week; my Aunt Viruchita did not answer four of my calls, on the fifth she told me that it was very early and that they were waiting for us at noon, and that she would send the driver. My Aunt Viruchita's driver was not as good as my Papá Manuelito's, one day I saw him "*haciendo taxi*"[27] on Arequipa Avenue in my Aunt Viruchita's car. I saw him in the luxurious black car with a little sign stuck on the front window that said: "Taxi." My Uncle Alberto's phone answered on the first ring. One of the cousins answered; as the voices of my three cousins were very similar, I tried calling my listener "primita" and as she responded with "Paquito" and not "Paquish," I realized that it was my cousin Mirelle. She just said: "Ay, Paquito, thank you very much, you better tell Delishita to call us later."

27 Moonlighting

The best part was when I dialed my Papá Manuelito's number, 223-0312, the number of the same line from which I was calling. There was no response, but after I kept trying I discovered that if I dialed the number and immediately hung up, the same phone would ring. So I had something new with which to entertain myself, apart from the invisible horse, for the rest of my stay.

Telephone similar to that of my Papá Manuelito's house on Santa Cruz 737 (Photo taken from the internet)

Lunch without stuffed avocado and chocolate

The huge residence of my Aunt Viruchita and my Aunt Elenita was located on the second floor above Bolognesi Plaza, right on the corner leading to the broad Avenue Brazil in the city of Lima. The mansion was huge because it consisted not only of the residence on the second floor, but also several stores for rent on the same floor both above the plaza and the first block of the avenue. When I was four years old, I loved to ring the doorbell of Aunt Viruchita's house. The doorbell consisted of a white button embedded in an ornate wrought iron frame painted black. The black and white of the button was in harmony, once the door opened revealing a beautiful staircase, with the white marble floors and a black painted wooden railing. In Cajamarca there were no doorbells. The gates of the colonial houses that I had visited; that of my Grandmother Pola, where we lived with my father, my three mothers, my brothers, the cook Juanachita and her mother Chochita, making four employees including Alicia and Herminia, added to Rosa and Micaela, Lorenzo and later our brother Zarquito Balarzo; that of my Papá Manuelito on the corner Jirón Amalia Puga; my Aunt Tulita's house on Jirón Comercio near the post office; my friend Mauelito Vilchez's house on Jose Galvez Street and Rafito Leon's on Jirón Amazonas, none had a doorbell, nor did the house of Uncle Leopoldo Rodriquez, Leopoldasho according to mi Papaíto, close to Manuelito's house around the corner from the cathedral. All of them had door knockers or rappers, which consisted of a hand or ring-shaped knocker of solid cast iron that were knocked against iron plates, not to have the doors opened, because if one wanted to, one could enter the houses simply by pushing them, but to advise the owners of the arrival of visitors.

Aunt Viruchita's steep white stairs reached about three meters. She climbed to the second floor taking more than twenty steps without resting. My mother climbed them with more than a little difficulty. I climbed them two steps at a time; I imagined that fat or heavy people would never be able to climb them or if they did climb them, it was likely that they would roll down from the second floor. My Aunt Viruchita, as always, was not ready when we arrived: it took her about twenty minutes to come out. My Aunt Elenita waited for us at the bottom of the stairs and after a warm embrace led us into the large living room. The furniture in the living room was identical to that of my Aunt Bebe Miranda's house on block 5 of Jirón Cajamarca in the city of the same name; I looked at my Aunt Elenita's face trying to guess if she would have my chocolate for after lunch, her sweet face told me nothing, but her lilting, affectionate speech confirmed that she would not fail.

My Aunt Viruchita came in coughing. She always coughed. My mother said it was because she smoked a lot. My aunt Yolita Cacho was also present. She accompanied the older aunts (not so old at that time) for many years. I went to the balcony to watch the cars driving around the Plaza Bolognesi; my entertainment consisted of counting the number of white and black cars that passed by making endless turns. There were more white cars than black cars; the black cars belonged to the rich, the white cars to the middle class. All my relatives had black cars. Suddenly, the bad news: there would be no lunch at my Aunt Viruchita's house. We would have lunch at El Nacional Restaurant, on the beach at La Herradura. So, I would not be enjoying my favorite appetizer: stuffed avocado with boiled potatoes, chicken, and mayonnaise.

The trip to the restaurant on the beach was made in the car driven by the ungracious driver. I was lucky enough to ride up front and see the city. I liked the city, but I didn't like walking along the Jirón de la Union in downtown Lima: the heat and the smell of the city of Lima's exhaust pipes gave me a headache. I liked the outdoors, like in Polloc or Cajamarca; going to the beach was fine. Two problems circulated in my head: the first was whether my Aunt Elenita would bring the chocolate to the beach, the second was knowing that I was sitting next to an unjust "*Saca vueltero*"[28] driver who used the car as a taxi for his own benefit. I was a good boy and could not stand having a scoundrel around me.

The restaurant was the most distinguished on the beach, white tablecloths and waiters dressed in tuxedos of the same color evidenced how fine the place was. My mother and my three aunts again ordered pisco sours and an ice cold soda for me. I was so hungry that I couldn't think anymore and without hesitation I asked Aunt Viruchita if she knew where the driver was with the car. She told me that he was parked and I answered: "What if he is '*haciendo taxi*'"? Aunt Yolita was also there and only managed to say: "Tomorrow I'll fire him." It was certain that she had already had similar experience with him.

Lunch was lively and full of delicacies. My aunt Vieruchita asked for a shrimp cocktail and they brought her prawns; my squeamish mother asked for several serrano dishes that were not available and ended up with two fried eggs over a small hill of rice; the two aunts ate fish and I had a sirloin steak with rice and mashed potatoes. At the end a chocolate came out of Aunt Elenita's purse. The heat of the Lima summer produced a soft chocolate stuck to the platinum paper. Smeared from having licked the platinum paper, I dirtied the white tablecloth and even three napkins; nobody noticed, the waiters, the maître d', my mother, and my two aunts were otherwise absorbed, concentrating on watching my Aunt Viruchita eating her fifth

28 Take a turn or run around

plate of prawns that had been served without greens (lettuce), because she only wanted to eat shrimp, in this case prawns smeared in *salsa golf* (a delicious, pink and smooth mixture of mayonnaise and tomato sauce), accompanied by pieces of avocado. In the end, she would pay the bill in cash, the bills all neatly tucked inside an envelope that Yolita had handed her under the table.

Iron door knocker similar to that of Grandma Pola's house on Cajamarca Street 628 (Photo taken from the internet)

La Joyita

The merciless days after the death of my Grandma Pola provoked the concern and action of all her loving relatives. My mother Delish was destroyed and with her my Mamita Perpetua. In order to avoid my mother's devastation, our beloved relatives prepared an endearing plan: twenty days in *La Joyita*[29] with Uncle Carlitos and Aunt Mary, plus twenty days in Lima with Papá Manuelito and Aunt Mary. Thanks to all of them, they were wonderful days! My mother was able to distract herself, keep company and find some relief, at least in part, because serious wounds to the heart never heal.

On the final stretch, the car turned on to a little road of find sand, the tires rested on the cushioning surface as it slid a few centimeters around the curves on the sandy surface. After a few surprising minutes the view of the green mountain range hand turned into that of the sandy coastline. La Joyita appeared, a little gift from heaven in the middle of the desert, an oasis of exterior beauty and interior harmony. It was six or seven o'clock in the evening. My Uncle Carlitos, my Aunt Mary, my adorable cousins Pamen and Fernandito, who was just entering childhood, were there to receive us.

Those who were not awaiting us were the actual owners of the house, its true guardians, the indomitable four harlequin-colored Great Danes, two of them white combined with black and the other two white and gray. There were also two other dogs, a bit smaller that, next to those Danes, went unnoticed. They stood like statues in the passageway, which could be described as an outdoor terrace. The four owners, were like precious pictures, they raised their ears, stood up,

29 Little Jewel

held their tails high, and ran to us. My Uncle Carlitos protected my mother who got out of the car first. The dogs obeyed only Uncle Carlitos. Already out of the car, I walked slowly towards the terrace and the four dogs, whose height allowed them to look at me face to face (I was eleven years old), they came rushing over, two of them aggressive and growling. I should let the readers know that my rural upbringing in Cajamarca taught me many ways to avoid dog bites; I have never suffered one despite how many times I have been exposed to such situations. After taking three or four steps, the dogs were just twenty centimeters away, but my acquired instincts made me stop instantly, I imitated a statue, and dogs never bite statues.

The days passed with walks with my cousins Pamen and Fernandito, Rafi and Alicia. We went to certain fields followed by the dogs. A lady's house served as a bodega and there, for a few coins, we drank *chicha morada*,[30] soft drinks and some fruit which tasted strange to me.

I don't know where she got them, nor how many she had, and I don't know how she dared: but my cousin Pamen got some cigarettes and together we learned to smoke, if you can call it smoking: light a cigarette, absorb the smoke only up to the mouth, then inflate the cheeks and expel the horrible volume of smoke that made us laugh and cough a lot.

Fernandito also wanted to smoke. He insisted by tugging on my forearm every time I raised the cigarette to my mouth. He preferred to ask me rather than his sister Pamen, who said no, yelling at him twice. The last time he insisted was when he pulled my hand that was holding the cigarette as it was already near my mouth. Then I turned my wrist and

30 A traditional Peruvian punch made with purple corn, pineapple skins, lime, cloves, cinnamon and sugar

the cigarette over and he, trying to draw on the awful butt, burned his lips. He jumped back and whimpered. It wasn't a burn, just a hot spot that burned his lips slightly, but it scared him enough to stop insisting. We didn't smoke every day it was just one or two times of pure childish play.

The lunches were quite fine. Uncle Carlitos was an instructive conversationalist, he gave advice and suggestions for good behavior in life to his children Tere, Pamen, and Fernandito, as well as to mi Rafi and me. He told us that people are known by their good behavior, that we are what we do, that if we exhibit good manners, we become well-mannered people, if we study in the afternoons and do our homework, we become good students, and that if a person lies he becomes a liar. He said that a teacher can "make taxi," but if he "makes taxi," he is a cab driver and is no longer a teacher. We are what we make of ourselves, he would tell us.

Walking through the house was torture: our bedroom was reached through a corridor that led right to the dining room, then the kitchen, a little farther to the back, always to the right, the family rooms, then a small courtyard and then, slightly to the left, the two rooms assigned to us visitors; that corridor and the courtyard, actually I would say the whole house, were the domain, the property of the dogs. The Great Danes knew, and then again, did not know us. My role as a statue was prodigious, but the dogs sniffing in my face, the growls in my ears and the fear I felt when I saw them approaching, did not cease to bother me. I moved like a statue around the house, stopping every few minutes, until the dogs were distracted, then moving two steps forward and so on. Delayed by having to avoid the dogs, I was always the last one to get to the bedroom, to the dining room or to watch TV in my Uncle Carlitos' study.

One of the luncheons was attended by my cousin Tere and her husband, a noisy cousin-in-law who was called "*El Flaco*"[31] who nevertheless later became very fat. Flaco used to say that he loved to drive fast, to travel to La Joyita by car, that his car was very fast, and that he drove at more than one hundred and twenty kilometers per hour or something like that. My Uncle Carlitos used to tell him, he used to tell us, because he was talking more to us than to his stubborn son-in-law, that prudence is indispensable in a sensible person, that whoever is not prudent is not sensible. Cousin Flaco insisted that it is better to go fast on the Pan-American Highway because if you go off the road, the car can get back on again meters ahead. If you go slowly the car will get stuck in the desert sand. Flaco didn't understand, didn't listen, nor did he want to understand. Maybe he just wanted to contradict his father-in-law or show off and appear very bold and brave. My Uncle Carlitos made efforts to explain to him that this was very dangerous. El Flaco would not allow himself be lose the debate, Uncle Carlitos told him and insisted, while looking more at Pamen and me, he thought that a rollover or a crash at high speed could be fatal. El Flaco hopingly gazed into our eyes in an effort to find an accomplice or at least some approval of his crazy thesis. He saw no danger, or if he did, he argued that the adrenaline caused by his actions behind the wheel was something we should admire. My Rafi opened his eyes in surprise and doubt, my mother was speechless, my cousin Tere was sweating, Pamen and I, as accomplices in cigarette smoking and other pranks, knowingly looked at each other, while my Aunt Mary softly rang the little bell for the *muchachas*[32] to

31 Skinny

32 Girls, the term used by the upper class in Peru to refer to the house help

come and to retrieve the empty plates and bring the stew that she offered with so much love.

In the evenings, it was very relaxing to watch television, even if it was only for a few brief moments. In my Uncle Carlitos' studio, before the sun set, during which the adults shared a few glasses of brandy while watching television. My Uncle Carlitos would ask my mother, "*Te provoca*[33] Terry Brandy, Delishita?" Terry was the brand, the phrase "te provoca" was simply an invitation repeated daily and always answered in the affirmative. So the adults would follow us children to my uncle's studio, they to drink brandy and talk, and us to watch TV. As we were sitting that afternoon on the fine beige leather furniture, all gathered there, my cousin Fernandito suddenly approached his father and said, in a tearful voice that we could all hear: "Papá, my cousin Paquish burned my lip," while making the face of a severely wounded victim. "How did he burn your lip Fernandito?" my uncle asked, raising his voice just a little bit more. "Smoking a cigarette," said Fernandito as he bit his upper lip, lowered his head and frowned. In a slightly louder voice, so we could all hear clearly, my Uncle Carlitos asked, "Does Paquito *fuma*?"[34] He pronounced the word "fuma" interrogatively and elongated the letter "u." I almost fell over backwards, my cousin Pamen passed the gum she was chewing between her molars sideways, blowing another bubble, my mother Delish again became mute, mi Rafi was playing with a little wagon and my Aunt Mary, observing my pregnant silence, stood up and left. My thoughts spun quickly. I wondered, "What will my Uncle Carlitos say now? Can time be turned back?" Uncle Carlitos called Pamen to his side, I don't

33 Literally "does it provoke you," meaning "would you like"

34 Smoke

know what he said to her, let alone what she answered. I only know that we never smoked again because whoever smokes is a smoker.

Gray Harlequin Great Dane, similar to the bravest at La Joyita (photo taken from the internet)

Panino, the black-eyed boy, receives a spanking

"From the window of an old hovel... / between the thick, leaden, greenish glass / a Salamancan girl with blond hair and eyes that look like pieces of the sky,... / every afternoon she watches the seminarians who go for a stroll in silence. She says nothing, only her chest tightens," and so does Paquito's chest as he tells this story:

Mi Coque, my endearing Coque, was mi Papaíto's cocky one, it seemed that there was a special connection between the two of them. For some reason which I don't understand, if mi Papaíto went out into the yard, Coque, only three years of age, would follow him; if Papaíto shaved, Coque would sit and watch him; he was his shadow.

Once he asked him: "What's your name, son?" "I call myself Coque Panino," he answered. Papaíto put his thumb on the palm of my Coque's little hand, closed his hand as if making a rooster's beak with his index finger and thumb, and with the help of his other hand, put his middle finger on the index finger, then the ring finger on top of the index finger and, finally, the pinky. He formed an "empanada," that is, a flour pastry in the shape of a crescent, filled with Cajamarcan cheese, which was prepared in the oven. That was a signal to decide: "Are we going to eat empanadas?" It was a sign of complicity, to go eat some empanadas on the sly, just the two of them. When Coque was hungry he would say: "Coque Panino" in order to say: "Coque wants empanada." As a result of this, he began to be called "panino" or, simply by the nickname: Panino.

Papaíto called him "mi Panino," his spoiled, adored one, his accomplice and companion, wherever he went, including the bank or the lounge of the Hotel de Turistas, where we had lunch.

Panino, the fourth among the twelve siblings, turned out to be the tallest as the years passed, the most intelligent and noble. He never fought with any of us in our little groups trying to win some game, jumping or spinning tops. He rode bareback —no saddles— he never considered a dog or horse to belong to him, everything of his was common property. At five or six years of age he read the catechism in one pass, practiced humility and saved me from going to hell: one day he spoke to me with such conviction, in the face of my doubts about the goodness of Christ, that he convinced me that to follow Jesus was not to expect receive goodness, but to give it, to practice it. I only answered: "You are going to heaven," adding, "you have already saved one soul, mine." He said nothing more, just looked at me and serenely finished his prayers, as usual, and fell asleep upstairs in the house in Polloc.

When he was ten years old, he was nominated to represent the school in the poetry contest, of which he became champion. We were looking for some music to accompany his poem. To my surprise he selected music for a procession of gladiators. As to my bewilderment towards such a choice, which I thought did not harmonize with the poem he was to recite: "The Seminarian with the Black Eyes," he told me: "It's for you, I know that you also want to recite and I have asked Professor Paredes to include you in the contest: you will recite the poem, "The Roman Circus."

The starry night crowned the sky above the courtyards of Cristo Rey School. The people had gathered: students and parents from all the boy's and girl's schools of the city of Cajamarca. They sat on more than one thousand chairs in front of the stage. The jury was composed of two high school teachers from the most representative schools in the city, the provincial

Director of Education, the Director Brother of the Cristo Rey School, and a representative of the parents. We, the participants, watched from behind the stage placed on a mezzanine in front of the large gathering. There were ten or twelve of us participants, the most colorful was a young boy from San Ramon School who would recite the poem "*Las Abandonadas*," it was known that the boy was masterful in recitation, that he used the entire stage from verse to verse and that his interpretation was formidable, and so it was that he was the third or fourth to go on stage.

How I pity the abandoned ones, who love believing that they were also loved, going through life weeping for a loved one, remembering a man and dragging along a child!

How are those, who tear the leaf from the tree and once they see it on the ground, will never retrieve it!

And those who knock down the green fruit with stones and throw it away after only one bite!

The abandoned ones are as fruit having fallen from the lush and tall tree of life; they are more than fallen, they are fruit felled by a false kiss, like a stone!

Throughout the streets roll those sad fruits, like squashed, shriveled apples, and on their poor, once robust bodies, they bear the indelible tooth-marks...

They have one of two paths to choose: the honorable path or the harem of vice; and in the midst of so many, many, many ordeals, there are still those who dare to speak to them of love!

Those magnates who can protect them, better that they
precipitate them, so that they might roll about more,
and there are even those who ultimately become their
executioner, wanting to squeeze from them
any juice they may yet have!

The abandoned ones are like the pulp that encloses a kiss and
incapacitates the embrace; if they yet have any juice,
pain sucks it out; they are sad pulp, the sad pulp of love!

When I meet them, their withered breasts
and worn faces are fraught with anguish,
and I think that they drag along with them their repentance:
a child who is the child of remorse...
A remorse trammeled by some hidden man,
who denies the child a roof and a name!

At the sight of those pale-haired children,
I would like to love them and be a parent to them.
The abandoned women fill me with sorrow,
because almost all of them are good women;
they are dried apples,
they are fruits fallen from the lush and tall tree of life.

There is no one to protect them, there is no one to pick them
up but the same wind that drags a leaf...
They march with their eyes fixed on the ground, tired of
looking in vain to the heavens!

For their deep sorrows, not even the Lord has pity, because of
these things... God knows nothing, and so go the poor,
weeping for a lost love, remembering a man
and dragging a child.

Of their deep sorrows, not even the Lord has pity, because of these things.... God knows nothing, and so go the poor, weeping for a sweetheart, remembering a man and dragging a child.

Julio Sesto

But Cristo Rey School's trump card was my brother Coque, he would be the last one to go out, it was a strategy designed by professor Paredes; I was hoping to be the revelation. My turn would be the seventh, it was a distracting stratagem for the jury and the audience, since I had the same last name as my brother Coque, already famous in the city, they would think that I was the best that our school had launched in the competition, and in the end it would be mi Coque, who should take the main prize.

I had rehearsed a thousand times, if not two thousand; I knew the poem by heart, the intonation with the pauses and the steps on stage. Trumpet music on the stage, the vinyl record was spinning to the sound of the gladiators' march: "Now Francisco Sáenz Ráez, first year high school student of Cristo Rey School," announced "El Loco Groso," the ceremony's host. Instantly my legs began to tremble as I bravely stood in front of the microphone and began: *"Marciano, badly closed the wounds / that he received yesterday in the torment, / present in the arena supported by two slaves; hesitant and tremolous...* And right there I saw that the fifth member of the jury, the representative of the parents, the one who had donated a bull for the raffle, was mi Papaíto.

My poem was beautiful, I knew it by heart, I had practiced the pauses, the intonation and all the mimicry, but I was not prepared to see my father in the jury.

Mi Coque acted as a prompter for my recitation, he was hidden in front of the stage and ready to remind me of any line in case I forgot. Everything was going quite well until a light shone on my father's face: I fell silent, livid. The pause went on too long; I hadn't forgotten the words, I was simply paralyzed. Mi Coque's low voice reminded me what I should say: "*Rubor sintiera, rubor sintiera,*" and believing that I had not heard him, in a louder voice, he insisted: "Rubor sintiera."

I did not hear anything, my thoughts flew through the clouds. I seemed to see my father's face and hear the laughter of Anitza Andabak, the girl I liked; it was a disaster. After a while I came to my senses and my memory returned, I continued until I finished reciting the poem, but it was too late: I had failed.

Marciano, the wounds that he received only
yesterday in the torment having poorly closed,
presented himself in the arena supported
by two slaves; hesitant and trembling.

His presence made a deep impression.
"Death to the Christian, the arsonist, the traitor!"
The crowd roared with a growl,
with a terrible roar, like thunder.

As if that insult had suddenly given life and
strength to the sick man, Marciano, upon
hearing this, stood up haughtily, released
himself from the hold of the servants, raised
his head, looked at the mob, and with rare vigor,
firmly and serenely crossing the arena,
arrived at the very foot of the royal platform.

It can be said that the courage of a man
before more than eighty thousand imposed fear,
because as Marciano advanced, the mob,
as if frightened by him went silent;
his words resounded throughout the
entire arena, reaching everyone:

"Cesar" he said, "he lies, he who affirms that
it was I who have set Rome afire.
If that brings me death, I shall die innocent.
I swear it before God who is listening to me.
But if my crime is that of being a Christian,
you do well to kill me, because it is true,
I believe in Jesus and practice His doctrine and
the best proof of my belief in Him, is that
instead of hating you, I forgive you!
And in dying for my faith, I die happy."

He said no more, after calmly and peacefully
finishing his speech, as at that very moment a huge
lion jumped into the arena shaking its curly mane.
The two advanced, one towards the other.
He with his arms folded across his chest,
the lion, the fierce beast, with fire pouring
from its eyes, opening its wide mouth with delight.

When they came face to face, they looked at each other,
and there was a moment when the lion, as if
troubled, in the presence of a man so serene...
made the indomitable brute ashamed
of attacking him, looking at him helplessly.
The silent scene lasted for a long time,
and at the end, the son of the desert's

fierceness won, he roared, crawled slowly
on the ground and with a leap he fell on his victim.

The people broke into thunderous applause.
The blood glistened, the sand was drenched
and even from the fight in tremendous
fury, Marciano with a cry of agony
"I forgive thee, Nero," he said again.

That cry was his last; the paw of the
ferocious animal cut his breath
and there the fight was over. Soon there was
nothing left of the whole thing but a few torn
and scattered garments on a body
also broken and undone, a fierce
beast drinking human blood
and a frenzied crowd applauding.

Juan Antonio Cavestany

Right after my intervention, it was mi Coque's turn, who came out tall and erect. He stood at the center of the stage, took the microphone and brought it to the very edge of the stage, adjusted the stand, gave a signal and the background music began. He looked up, as if contemplating the window of a mansion, which from the second floor, an evening tear was being shed. The crowd before the stage was not breathing, or at least not a murmur could be heard.

From the window of an old hut, open in summer,
closed in winter by greenish, thickly leaded glass,
a Salamancan woman with blond hair

and eyes that look like pieces of the sky,
her sewing mingled with prayer,
silently watches every afternoon
the seminarians as they go for a walk.
She lowers her head, without raising her body,
they march in two slow and austere rows,
with no cheerful sign upon their black robes,
beyond the red scarves that girdle their necks,
which fall at their backs almost touching the ground.

One seminarian, among them all,
marches always erect, with a resolute air.
The black cassock outlines his body,
gallant and graceful, flexible and slender.
He walks alone, stealthily, and the clergymen
observe his glances with fear.

From the street he glimpses the blond-haired
Salamancan woman in the distance,
he looks at her very fixedly, with an intense gaze.
And as he passes by, she leaves him with
the memory of that look in her blue eyes.

Monotonously and slowly the time passes
and the summer dies and then the autumn
with its leaden winter afternoons arrives.
From the window of the old hovel
always alone and sad, praying and sewing,
The blond-haired Salamanca girl watches
every afternoon as the seminarians silently pass by.
But she doesn't see them all; she only sees one,
her black-eyed seminarian.

Each time he passes by, dashing and slender,
he observes the girl who yearns for that body
instead the of cassock, the martial harness.
When he fixes his open eyes on her with
lively and daring glances of fire,
he seems to say: I love you, I love you!
I can't be a priest! I can't be a priest!
If I am not to be yours I will die, I will die, I will die!
Then the girl's chest tightens, her work is halted,
and she forgets her prayers,
and the black-eyed seminarian
lives alone in her thoughts.

On a rainy winter morning
the girl, who was joyfully jumping out of bed
heard the sad chants and funeral prayers;
a funeral was passing along the narrow street.
A seminarian was undoubtedly the deceased
as four carried the coffin on their shoulders
with the red scarf, and black hood covering the lid.
With their hoarse voices the clergymen sang,
the seminarians went in silence,
always in two rows towards the cemetery
as in the afternoons when going for their walk.
The anguished girl watched the procession;
she knew them all by sight. . .
Only, only the seminarian with the
black eyes was missing among them.

The years passed by, a long time passed...
and there, at the window of the old hovel,
a poor old woman with white hair,
leathery complexion and stooped body,

As her sewing mingles with prayers,
every evening she sees the seminarians pass by in silence.
She looks at them, and when she sees them,
her blue eyes, now sad and dead,
shed silent tears, silent tears of ice.
Alone, old and sad, she still holds the memory
of the seminarian with the black eyes.

Miguel Tramos Carrion

He rose, raised his arms, cried, held fast, was moved, and finished amid the applause.

The jury took a long time to deliberate. I knew I would be in last place.

Mi Coque had closed the show, focused himself on chatting with friends, he was already in another world, he did not care about the result, rather, he enjoyed the process, the actual world around him; he forgot the past, he did not care about the future. That attitude infected me and we went, with Papaíto's tips, to eat empanadas sold by a boy from his little basket.

The result was as follows, the influence of the fifth member of the jury was evident: First place and gold medal for "*El Seminarista de los Ojos Negros*;" second place and silver medal for "*Las Abandonadas*," and third place and bronze medal for "*El Circo Romano*." With all that has just been described, the reader should not come away believing that mi Coque was a saint nor a quiet man. It is worth mentioning that one day he acquired, thanks to his own actions, the nickname of *el Zurrao*: at thirteen years of age. He had fallen in love with a girl from Trujillo, named Carolina, whom we met during the summer trip of that same year, at the house of my Bazán Pinillos cousins, near Huanchaco Beach.

One Saturday in September, very early, before six o'clock in the morning, we set out on my little motorcycle. It was a blue, 100cc Honda, it was not red because that was the color of the devil, according to mi Mamita Perpetua, who obliged me to receive this sky-colored gift from mi Delish. I was the pilot and mi Coque was the passenger who, carrying a one gallon can full of gasoline which we never used, had the job of refueling. Without a driver's license, without protective helmets and without our parents' permission or knowledge, we set off for the spring festival at in the city of Trujillo. The objective was to see the spring celebrations, attend a party at Carolina's house and then to undertake the return trip to Cajamarca on Sunday afternoon; as there were so many of us siblings, no one would notice our absence.

Before seven in the morning, at the top of Gavilan hill, we crossed paths with my uncle Alex Bisiak who was coming up from the coast and to whom we waved from the motorcycle. He looked at us with surprise and only managed to shake his head and wave back. He thought we were only going to the small town of San Juan. Indeed, after an hour we were leaving San Juan. Mi Coque's arms could no longer support the weight of the gas can. The tank of the motorcycle was full, so we hid the gas can full of fuel under cover, beneath a mound of earth and stones, and put a wooden cross on it to identify the place upon our return.

The trip took us until late at night, I don't remember what we had for lunch, nor where. At six thirty in the evening, the sun was setting, driving the motorbike on the road was very dangerous – the lights of the trucks blinded us. We decided to follow a slow truck, so we arrived in Trujillo at Carolina's party at about nine o'clock that night, after taking a shower at Irmita Cruzado's house, a former collaborator of my Aunt Viruchita and a friend of my mother Delish, on España Avenue 2671.

The party that night at Carolina's house was fun, but nothing too special to mention. The parade on Sunday morning left us astonished, we were especially impressed by the North American majorettes who threw their batons to the skies and in little turns caught them, harmoniously following the march to the beat of the band of musicians, also the *marineras* that repeated two or three songs. The *caballos de paso*, the *chalanes* and the *amazonas*, the beauty queens: everything was sensational.[35]

We had to leave before one o'clock in the afternoon. I did it alone, without my co-pilot: Coque decided to stay two more days.

On Monday morning, already back in Cajamarca, all of us older children left for school: mi Caly to kindergarten and Abeta and Rafi to elementary school. My Mamaíta counted heads three times, she was missing one: Coque Panino was not there. She panicked, called Papaíto, who went to the police. I, lips zipped, would never rat on a fellow adventurer. We left for school, and when we returned home the house was in chaos: phone calls, police, even bums from the city were paraded out to be asked they knew anything about the missing fugitive. It took two days: on Tuesday afternoon Coque showed up at the Diaz & Diaz transport schedule office. He received a *zurra*[36] at the door of the station, then was chased by Papaíto through the city's Plaza de Armas, it was news all over town.

That's how my Coque took on his new nickname, given by Luis, *el Chanca, Centurión*, from then on his nickname was *el Zurrao*.

---

35 Marinero means sailor, *Marinera*, in Peru, is a traditional folk music and dance. Here "*manineras*" refers to the performers as does "*chalanes*" to the riders of the *caballos de paso*, and "*amazonas*" to those performing the music and dance of that region

36 Spanking

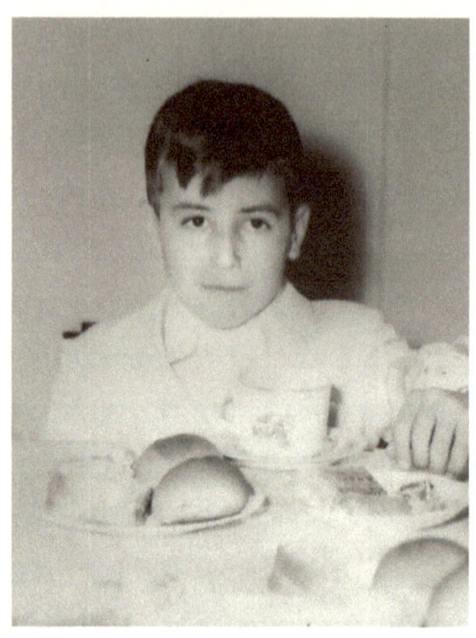

Coque Panino 8 years old at his first communion

Coque at 15

Coque at 20 years old, shortly before his death, with Kiko my little brother. He left his university studies for a year in order to help our father

Some jewels to fall in love with

Delishita, excited, encouraged by Mamaíta, and in the company of us all, set out on a horseback ride from Polloc to Namora. The first leg of the journey would take us about two hours, so we had to leave early at about six in the morning. The troop was very unique: Mamaíta on the mare Primavera, her favorite companion; Delishita on the very docile Blanquita, Joaquin's mare, mi Manuel on La Castaña; Tringo on the mare Perla, the very tall and second daughter of Mensajera; mi Coque on Blanca Luz, mi Pepe on the mare Baya; Zarquito on the very fat and wide-legged Señora López – whose name or nickname we gave inspired by Mamaíta's hairdresser who groomed from her shop on Lima Street in front of the Hotel de Turistas in the city of Cajamarca in the early 1960s – mi Chini rode Golondrina, the eldest daughter of Mensajera, and el niño Paquito guided his beloved mount, the mare Chuña, followed by the dogs of the hacienda, of which there were about six, not counting the small breed dogs that never went out. We head out to that town that makes you fall in love.

The plan was to arrive at Chuchún – the immense hacienda that, in its 11,000 hectares, surpassed Polloc's 600, and that witnessed the birth of my Grandmother Pola –, visit the church, have breakfast with Donatila, the Dona, until ten o'clock in the morning at the latest; then continue on to Namora, in a journey that would take us three additional hours, until we arrived to sing with my aunt Olguita Bueno Cacho and my cousins Adolfito and Esperancita Anamorín Bueno, in order to, finally, after this long and pleasant journey, embark on the return trip. A difficult task, unanticipated in its distance and difficulty.

In effect, we left before six o'clock in the morning, eager to see Aunt Olguita. The early morning crowing of the roosters and the barking of the dogs at the passing of the fighting bulls coming from La Pauea (a Cajamarcan cattle ranch) woke us up very early. The six fighting bulls, surrounded by oxen and cows to calm them down, and riders on horseback with long whips, forced us to close the gates to the house in front of it the barbed wire fences of the paddocks facing the church.

From the windows of the second floor, frightened as always when the bulls passed through Polloc, we watched the caravan that surely was heading to the festivities of Celendín. We feared the passing of the intense bulls because of Papaíto's warnings, Mamaíta's fears, and the emotional impact that the fight between our bulls left on us a short time previous.

That was the time when our bull Rícard escaped from his pen and fought with the larger one named Americano, both of them very big (the first one weighing 800 kilos and the second one about a ton), not fighting bulls, but a Holstein dairy breed. Rícard and Americano were brought from Holland with a small batch of 12 heifers that were very resistant to the Andean climate, not like the 40 American cows that my father brought years later from the Pabst ranch in the United States, which died quickly and caused us so much grief.

The fight between the bulls was terrible, it took the effort of 30 laborers to separate the animals using ropes around their necks and more than 100 buckets of ice cold water thrown on their heads.

Rícard was beautiful in appearance, black and precious; he was the champion of the breed in the regional fair of Cajamarca, back in 1957 or 1958. The destruction of the patio, the hay barn door, the pillars of the offices, the storage shed, and Mamaíta's garden and fence were tremendous; as were the injuries caused to Americano, a huge bull weighing a ton, who was dehorned, by those of Rícard, who was in turn left lame for a long time in his left leg, in addition to other wounds inflicted upon him. The fury of the bulls, the screams of the women and the anguish of Papaíto frightened us so much that our nightmares of lions chasing us vanished in the face of those of the bulls escaping from their pens for a very long time.

Imagine, reader, that once, after this distressing event, when I was about four or five years old, I could not control my horse while returning to the ranch and, still mounted, it led me to Rícard's corral, which was open for cleaning. The horse's desire was to eat the best hay that was being served to the king of Polloc's cattle. I tugged on the reins of this horse who, out of a craving for fresh grass, had become an untamed beast, but my strength was not enough: driven by its instinct, I ended up at the very far end of the corral. My horse started to eat from the feed bin and I jumped off of her; terrified and frightened, with my heart pounding and without caring about the wet manure or the dirty straw. I ran out of there. The bull was not there: three employees had taken him, held with ropes from the ring of his nose and his neck, to bathe him in the irrigation ditch. I ran to the entrance of the passage to the house, closed all the doors behind me, bolted to the kitchen, slammed the doors shut and grabbed Mamaíta's legs.

We took the road to the *pampa*[37] of Polloc, high in the hills behind the hacienda house. The steep climb was easy to take, on the way back we had to skirt that steep climb or get off our horses to avoid falling face first over the heads of the animals, as mi Chini and Caly had from the white donkey a few years later.

We took the road and then the bridle path until we reached the top of the sheep pasture. From there at a hurried pace along the road. In two hours we were approaching Chuchún; we arrived at the house of the Dona, which was in a green esplanade that consisted of a large garden of green grass in

37 High plain

front of the old church. Next to it was the hacienda house, which at that time appeared semi-destroyed.

Before the succulent and very affectionately served breakfast, as corresponds any the visit with our beloved Delita, after so many years and with so many memories, we visited the place where my Grandmother Pola was born; it was a room facing a small patio in the old house. We entered the old church, the image of the Virgin of Chuchún looked upon us with pleasure and affection, three Hail Maries gave us her blessing before visiting the bell tower from where *Loquito*[38] José, who years ago, for a tip of only two peseta coins, would ring the bells for the dead so that their souls could escape purgatory.

More than 200 year old image of the Virgin of Chuchún. (Today in Paquito's house)

The prosperity and fortune of the Dona was evident, who that day lavished us with guinea pig stew, boiled potatoes, beans, corn, and portions of lamb and duck meat. Breakfast was served in the garden, sitting on the ground on our ponchos and not in the dining room of the old house that held so

38 Little crazy

many dear thoughts, like the memory of Loquito José himself asking his señora for eggs under the table.

After breakfast, we immediately went to visit the playground of mi Delish and her siblings from when they were children. The place was around the Talalán. The Talalán was a magical place that consisted of a large entrance to a well of slightly murky water. My Delishita took a stone, threw it into the well; the instant the stone hit the water, the well said: "Splash." After a short silence, the well spoke again and said, "Talalán.

We all repeated the operation many times, well away from the Talalán so as not to fall in: we threw many stones and the well, each time, after a pause, always answered: "Talalán, talalán, talalán."

The muddy ascent – full of stones of all sizes, some embedded in the mud and others loose – winding and dangerous to cross the mountain range, was very exciting. Not so were the descents from the hills and the ravines formed by the waters that descended from the *jalcas*.[39] Sometimes during the descents, if they were very steep and slippery because of the mud, we had to get off the horses to avoid falling. The rider who had the hardest job was me, because, riding my stubborn mare named Chuña, I could do nothing, no matter how hard I pulled her, spurred her with my heels, braked, or indicated her to go one way, she would go the other, never obeying.

After three long hours, without the dogs that had returned home once they noticed how far away our destination lay, we arrived to Namora, to its beautiful plaza and hidden corners. We stopped at a bodega to have a soda. The one who surprised us this time was mi Pepe, who saw two friends who had told him they were going on a trip to Lima, but he found them in

39 Mountain tops

that place. They hid themselves so as not to be caught outside the capital; but mi Pepe spotted her in Namora and almost sighed, at his tender age his heart was already beating fast at the sight of one of the two girls in that place where visitors fall in love. El Zarquito did the same, and it occurred to me that his intentions were the same but directed to the other girl we encountered there.

Plaza de Armas of Namora today (photo taken from the internet)

We mounted the horses and in 20 minutes we arrived at La Perla, Aunt Olguita's paradisiacal place. Lunch with *humitas*[40] and steak was accompanied by *chicha de jora*,[41] guitars and *cajon*.[42] Olguita's voice sounded powerful and intoned. However, her passion for singing and camaraderie stood out more, not because the former was not magnificent, but because the latter, always in her, was extraordinary. The "little Amorin cousins," as my Delish used to call them, were and still are as affectionate as their mother. The

40 Fresh corn pounded to a paste, wrapped in a corn husk, and slowly steamed or boiled

41 A drink made from fermented corn

42 Percussion instrument consisting of a wooden box – a national treasure which is now played all around the world

same goes for my cousins and grand cousins of Aunt Olguita, they truly are jewels.

Facade of the remodeled house in La Perla (photo taken from the internet)

PART TWO

Land, children, land

At Papá Manuelito's house in 1958, when I was four years old, I discovered that the phone rang, it rang by itself without someone calling from outside, from another line. If you dialed the same number of the line you were calling from, the phone would ring. So what was the secret? Call your own number and immediately hang up the handset on the arm that went up and down with the weight of the handset and opened or closed the phone line. Then run and hide, waiting for someone in the house to vainly answer the phone and then laughing on the sly. This I did over and over again, I would dial Papá Manuelito's number and hang up immediately, so the phone would ring several, many times.

I had dialed 2230312 and hung up immediately, already for the seventh or eighth time, the phone rang and, the door of my Papá Manuelito's study, who was gathered with his three sons: Uncle Carlitos, Uncle Luchito and Uncle Jaimito in a meeting of men, of adults, it was a conclave between the protective father and the dedicated sons; Papá Manuelito's door was constantly opening and closing as he came out to see why the phone was ringing so many times. I hid behind the door of the small bathroom near the stairs, it was a white tiled bathroom with black trim which gave it a very elegant tone. When Papá Manuelito turned his eyes towards the main room, I ran and entered to where the desk was with the door half open, the three uncles were silent, as if they were meditating. By their faces I thought they had received a reprimand. I stood near the door within view of the three of them. They did not notice me, as they were facing the other way. I took the precaution of moving behind the door when Papá Manuelito came back in, closed the door and I remained inside the room. He went straight to his desk, sat down on the swivel chair, took a pen, a fountain pen they called it, the triangular tip of it in an opaque glass pommel filled with liquid ink, and signed a piece of paper.

He stood up, the three sons also stood up practically at the same time, they stood up as if propelled by three springs, as if they were rehearsed. He looked them in the eyes and said, shaking the paper: "Land sons" and repeated: "Land." Since then I've only put my money, not in land because I cannot afford it, but having learned the advice, I only invest in real estate.

The angry peacock

Sunbathing in the back garden of my Papá Manuelito's house was magnificent. The back part of the house at Santa Cruz 737 was very beautiful: the leafy trees at the back of the mansion kept company in harmonious guard to that beautiful Eden; smaller trees and beautiful plants full of flowers forested the place, surrounding that paradise with leaves in a celebration of nature. The trees at the back of the garden, those majestic giants, watched over the beauty there, preventing the sun's rays from passing for a just few hours each day as the afternoon slowly fell.

During the mornings, at noon, and in the early evening hours, the sun warmed the green grass, flowers and roses that surrounded this paradise. This was my Aunt Teresita's garden. Walking, sitting in the sun or lying on the well-kept lawn were the delights most enjoyed by my mother Delish (who was always sensitive to chill air), mi Mamita Perpetua and Alicia.

However, the most beautiful thing in that splendid place was a beautiful peacock: it spread its tail and wings, raised its head, beautiful, beautiful! It adorned and decorated the garden, transforming the whole place into a spectacle worthy of a watercolor painting. Without a doubt, my Aunt Teresita's peacock was the most beautiful bird in the world.

Three serranas were sunbathing, a mischievous child was fluttering around – that was me at only four years of age; the sun was setting spectacularly, the mysterious shadows of the trees were slowly approaching and a beautiful peacock was opening its wings, portentous, unfurling its symmetrical multicolored fan-shaped tail, and in his haughty gait, he spun like the lord and master of the garden. Such was the picture in the orchard of Papá Manuelito and Aunt Teresita's house in the summer of 1958.

While the three ladies were sunbathing, Paquito, a bit bored, was looking for fun: what more fun could there be for me than to go and annoy the prince of the garden! Papá Manuelito had already warned me that the peacock didn't like any competitors. Even so, I tried to imitate him by opening my arms, raising my jaw horizontally and walking sideways. Such was the imitation that the peacock felt that someone more beautiful was approaching him, and coming quite close, invading his space, his imperial territory. I don't remember anything else: I only saw the once beautiful animal turn into a horrible creature jumping on me, he gave me a tremendous push with his body and wings; I don't know if it was with his right foot or with his left foot with which he unloaded a kick in my little left eye. As best I could, I ran away, I did not cry. I never cried as a child, or at least I think so. One of its horrifying feet left me with a swollen and bruised eye for several days.

My Mamita Perpetua jumped on the peacock, my mother Delish ran to the backyard and came back with a broom, Alicia screamed and my Aunt Teresita ran down from the second floor, alarmed with so much screaming; Papito Manuelito was not home. Belladonna ointment and vanilla ice cream soothed my pain and anxiety, but not my indignation. The last memory I have of that bird was the words of my Aunt Teresita: "Don't ever mess with the peacock again."

Preparations for lunch in a palace

The logic was as follows: my Papá Manuelito was a close friend of the President of the Republic of Peru, Mr. Manuel Prado Ugarteche. My Papá Manuelito was my godfather, I was staying at his house, and since I was a good and obedient boy, ergo, I was invited to the Governmental Palace to have lunch with President Prado. Additionally, the invitation was extended to my mother Delish, my Papá Manuelito and my Aunt Teresita. At first I was not enthusiastic about the invitation, because I would have to leave my invisible horse at home and I would also miss the adventures of Rin–Tin–Tin and Furia.

My mother's preparations began five or six days before the invitation: we went to the Boza Galleries, which were in the center of the city within the first blocks of the Jirón de la Union, near the Plaza San Martin and a few blocks from the Plaza Mayor or Plaza de Armas of Lima. The Jirón de la Union was the most solemn passage of the city, where the most select ladies, elegant gentlemen and the middle classes who could not acquire products directly on trips abroad, strolled and shopped. However, the most important thing for those who went to the Jirón de la Union was not to go shopping but to see their peers, to see and be seen. For my mother Delish the goal was to buy a dress elegant and appropriate enough to meet the President of the Republic and Senator Manuel Cacho–Sousa. The dress had to be demure, elegant, and inexpensive – a rather difficult mission, although not impossible if one kept in mind the three sayings I've known since I was a child from my mother's lessons, my grandmother Pola: "The cassock does not make the monk," "everything fits a good model" and "the essence of perfume comes in small a bottle." So my mother, with these three sayings in mind, rushed to the Boza Galleries, dragging me by one arm, with her black purse hanging from the other, and her eyes fixed on the window of a store on the second floor.

For me, a four year old boy, going out for lady's shopping was always an unlivable ordeal; the heat of the city, the carbon monoxide emanating from the exhaust of the buses and cars, coupled with my mother's slow pace, gave me an unbearable headache; the soporific humid air of Lima was not for me. Fortunately, the Boza Galleries had amazing escalators ascending to the second floor, those stairs were my salvation: they were amazing, they went up so slowly that I could jump to the first step from the second floor and after only two minutes I could jump from that same step to the second floor again, fast enough to thrill a four year old boy from Cajamarca who had never seen anything like them before – remember that my passion was jumping. I climbed them more than 50 times, once I made those endless mechanical ascents and descended physically via the cement stairs that began at the end of the left corridor, I discovered that the most exciting thing was to go down the up escalators; there was no better way to do it than on horseback, so I mounted my invisible horse, and from trot to trot and jump to jump, I went up and down the stairs of the Boza Galleries an infinite number of times.

With my mother's little black dress now in a plastic bag, my headache attenuated, but very thirsty, we walked along the busy Jirón in the direction of the Plaza Mayor.

A place called Botica Francesa, in the fourth block of the Jirón de la Union, which since 1824 offered Italian style sorbets, rewarded my enormous sacrifice of enduring the sun, coping with the tedium and cheating the headache.

The upper classes of Lima used to go to the Botica Francesa not only to buy their medicines, but also to enjoy cakes and *gelatos*. For me the latter meant everything: in Cajamarca ice cream was only sold between the months of June and August, when a refrigerated truck of the Donofrio brand would gloriously burst into the Plaza de Armas on Sundays and sell these desserts, especially an ice cream called Alaska, which had the parallel lined shapes of a small brick was my favorite: it consisted of vanilla cream surrounded by a thin layer of chocolate and the whole thing tasted delicious, although it cost an amount of money that I didn't always have. I remember that I liked them so much that I once asked myself: "When will I grow up and have enough money to eat all the ice cream I want? This motivation has always driven me to surpass myself to be able to buy all the ice cream I could ever desire.

It was about eleven o'clock in the morning when a huge gelato quenched my craving, my hunger and my headaches; however, to my regret, my mother Delish had yet to buy her shoes; we agreed that while she bought the shoes in an elegant store nearby, I would play in the gardens of the small plaza that had the statue of Francisco Pizarro mounted on a horse. I can only say that it was wonderful to climb on the back of the conquistador, too bad that this was not to the liking a uniformed guard who returned me by the ears to the shoe store.

Lunch at the palace

I never went to the Government Palace; I never went to lunch with the President of the Republic, Manuel Prado Ugarteche, a close friend of my godfather; I was never invited; futhermore, I was not invited to a lunch to which my Papá Manuelito, my mother Delish and my Aunt Teresita had been. I don't know why at the age of four I heard there was a luncheon, I don't know why it occurred to me that the invitation was for me.

It was an elegant dinner at the Government Palace, it started at seven o'clock at night, after they took me to bed and left me at home asleep. My mother went to the Government Palace to dine with the President of the Republic and to show off her attire bought in the Jirón de La Unión. The passages and halls of the Palace of Government, the words of the president, the cuisine and the beautiful Golden Hall, I only knew of them by hearsay the following day.

La Nena

To make up for my absence at the dinner I missed at the Government Palace with the President of the Republic, my Papá Manuelito invited me to dinner at La Nena, his small farm in the outskirts of Lima. La Nena was a few kilometers from the central highway, which leads to the lands of Junín in the highlands of Peru, it was the smallest of Papá Manuelito's farms. I don't know if it was in Chosica or Chaclacayo, I only know that it was a beautiful place. That time the invitation was at night. Entering La Nena was a wonderful experience for me when I was four years old. To my mind I was the principle guest, the second was President Prado.

My Papito Manuelito's elegant car drove him, my Aunt Teresita, my mother Delish and me to this beautiful place at about seven o'clock in the evening, when the stars were beginning to peek through high in the heavens, and I could see them with my head out of the window and my neck twisted looking to infinity. The main guest, me, was in the front seat of the car driven by the best of the drivers, the one who never spoke, the one who drove so smoothly and kept the car in perfectly maintained and clean condition.

The car pulled over to the right hand side, a huge gleaming wooden gate opened with just two honks of the car, the road to the house was illuminated with little yellow lights on the sides of the road between white painted pebbles, and other green florescent lights spread beautifully over the treetops. The view was beautiful, the driver guessed my thoughts and slowed down, it was slow, very slow, I was enraptured, contemplating the little lights, the trees and in the background the beautifully lit house.

The dinner was very lively, other families were invited, I do not know if there were six or eight more people; my mother Delia held her glass with only two fingers, I knew how to handle the silver cutlery and could choose which of them corresponded to each dish. I knew how to distinguish the wine glass, – the smallest, the champagne glass – the tallest and the fresh water glass – the largest and fattest. I was quite a charming lad. I followed the conversation with interest: Italian banks, agricultural feudatories or property taxes, it was all most conciliatory, no one argued or contradicted President Prado. The blancmange, brought from *La Quispa*,[43] sweet and soft, was the best, although it heralded the end of the gathering. It was about eleven o'clock at night and I had to go to sleep.

President Prado was very nice, he knew how to maintain a high level conversation; during the tea and coffee, standing on the terrace overlooking the sloping field, I asked him if he was happy being president, to which he replied that he was happy to have good friends and asked if I wanted to be his friend. In a polite manner I told him quite high-mindedly, "Friends have to see each other very often and I won't be able to see you, I live in Cajamarca." "You will have to come, then, often," he told me. I answered: "It would be better for you to come, at least once, because I don't have that much money or time." My friend Manuel did not say anything else, I think he remained resentful because I never saw him come to Cajamarca. I preferred to continue contemplating the beautiful landscapes of La Nena from the loft of the terrace which allowed me to observe the countryside leaning towards the gleaming wooden gate.

43 A hacienda in Cajamarca

A pistol for a child

It was only a short distance from my Papá Manuelito's house to my Grandfather Ernesto's. From the 7th block of Jirón Santa Cruz on, all you had to do was go out of the big door, turn right, go to the corner and cross the street to the left, walk forty steps, and you were at Huayna Capac 1253, the house of my grandfather, my mother Mechita's father.

Ernesto Ráez Cisneros, General of the Peruvian Army – Division General – my mother was quick to say in order to highlight his trajectory, was a tough, serious character and, according to many, very strict and severe, that is to say, difficult to get along with.

When I was four years old, I had agreed, with only a phone call, to go to lunch at my grandfather's house, my Grandfather Ernesto. Faithfully fulfilling my commitments, at half past twelve o'clock that afternoon in 1958, I shined my little shoes, combed my hair and then washed my face and hands with soap and water, just as the *Pimpón*[44] doll had taught me. Without saying goodbye or informing anyone of my departure, I left for my grandfather's house.

As soon as I rang the doorbell, Neno, my grandfather's wife, greeted me in gym clothes. She led me to the garden of the house where my grandfather was whistling to a beautiful yellow canary, imprisoned in a white cage. She - mi Neno - continued spinning around, turning her body as she spun across the floor of the large main room, eager to maintain her slender form and ingratiate the general.

They were waiting for my mother Delish, also for lunch, but my mother did not arrive, they called her on the phone

44 An animated character created in Chile

and she told them that she did not know where I was. She was desperate, she made a fuss before everyone in my Papá Manuelito's house; she even called the police, to whom she assured I had been kidnapped and that the proof was the little comb thrown down in the bathroom. Once the situation was clarified, she later denounced me to my grandfather during lunch, she accused me of being naughty and spoiled for not telling her where I was. My grandfather, who had a reputation for sternness, simply assessed the situation by telling her: "He came to visit me, I am his grandfather and this young man already had an appointment."

During lunch, the head of the family, being the general he was, sat down at the head of the aluminum table, placed his elbows on the large glass table top which was decorated with napkin holders, a pitcher of fresh water and glasses, all decorated with green ribbons of the same material. My grandfather was served only with fresh a salad and boiled vegetables of all colors. For my mother and me, there was a vegetable soup that could be smelled from five meters away. It smelled strong, it smelled like boiled vegetables that were uneatable for a snobby little kid like me. Accustomed to stuffed avocado and fried eggs over steak on white rice, I heroically swallowed the vegetable soup without chewing any of it and sighing for God's mercy. As I had finished the soup so quickly, they assumed I liked it and offered me a second helping, to which, standing up and raising both hands in a high sign, I answered: "No, no;" after apologizing for the clumsiness of my answer, I enjoyed a main dish of lasagna for the first time in my life. There was no dessert, only fruit.

My dour grandfather did not speak at all during lunch, he just ate hurriedly, like someone fulfilling a mission: nothing disturbed him, he was just doing his duty, and that was to eat, and to do so healthily and quickly. The conversation between my mother and mi Neno was nothing special, nothing worth remembering anyway. At the end of lunch my grandfather stood up and went to his desk, he didn't say anything: neither thank you nor see you soon. His very personal refuge, his desk, was located behind the front door to the left, behind a door that was always closed and that always hid my grandfather sitting at his desk with his eyes on his papers, but near the front door to keep an eye on who was entering or leaving the house.

My mother, mi Neno and I went to the main dining room to peruse the beautiful and large silverware, most of which was purchased as wedding gifts. Tired of seeing so much silverware and glassware, I ran out to watch my *abuelito*[45] at work.

How strange lunch was at my abuelito's house! Later my Mamita Perpetua told me that this is how you eat in order to live a hundred years. I didn't want to live a hundred years, I just wanted to grow up and be the size of my grandfather who was very tall; the Ráez were taller than the Sáenz and the Cacho, not so as tall to reach six feet, but they were over five foot-eight.

I carefully and quietly opened the brass handles and then pushed open the door to my grandfather's study, which was closed, as usual; I saw him sitting behind his desk, crying as he looked at some photographs showing his parents and others of some men parading. I thought he didn't know I was there, but he said, "Come in, grandson," as he wiped away a tear with one of his fingers. Instantly he opened one of the drawers.

He opened the first drawer on the left of his huge light brown, shiny wooden cabinet. He took out a white handkerchief to dry his last tears, and a slim wallet, then took out a bill to tip me – I think it was the first time I had ever

45 Abuelo - grandfather

had a bill in my hands. A bill in my hands and it was mine, just for me!

I was not impressed by the bill so much as I was by his sweet words: "Don't be scared, my grandson, this is how I am, I love you very much," he told me, and he extended me the bill that I kept in the right back pocket of my pants and that I would never know about again, until mi Mamita Perpetua showed it to me, disintegrated, after having washed my pants. I didn't have the bill nor its returns, but I do have the sweet memory of the words and the look of my grandfather Ernesto, who was so good.

My grandfather, Major General – Artillery Division, sword of honor, accused of plotting the coup against President Odría, in rebellion with his friend Zenón Noriega, deported and later elected Senator of the Republic, famous for his strictness and severity – sweetly told me that he loved me.

There is something else to tell here, guess what I saw?

In the corner of the drawer, right there, I saw a pistol. The embossed steel of the barrel and slide made it look beautiful. It was small, .25 caliber, had a gleaming mother-of-pearl grip; the trigger, barrel and slide were also of gleaming metal. Its shape, its profile, the design if you will, and its thickness were perfect. It struck me as being ideal, ideal in its size, its beauty, and the function it could have in my hands, and in my possession. I dreamed of surpassing my father and his little .22 caliber pistol in scaring the pigs and donkeys that invaded Polloc's paddocks. Even more, I had the illusion of shooting the intrusive pigs that with their drool, contaminating the barley fields and that hungrily ate the rye wheat that my father sowed and cared for with so much care.

Years later, many years later, after the death of my grandfather that gun was given to me by mi Neno saying:

"Your abuelito left this pistol for you." I am sure that my grandfather, that afternoon after lunch, read my eyes, interpreted my wish and remembered me. Because my grandfather Ernesto was so good.

Precious .25 calibre pistol, similar to that of my Grandfather Ernesto

The little black watch

The little black watch was given to me by my Papá Manuelito from one of his trips to Cajamarca; it was small, but not as small as a woman's watch. It was as black as the strap that danced on my wrist, it told the time, although I did not know how to tell the time, since I was only four years old.

He gave it to me in the courtyard of my grandmother's house, on Jirón Cajamarca 628, where we twelve siblings would live so happily. I loved that gift from my Papá Manuelito; I was the happiest child in the house; I was the only child who had a watch. I took so much care of the little watch that I am very sad to remember that at some point I lost it, maybe it got damaged, but I am sure that since I was very naughty, it didn't last me more than a month.

The most beautiful house in the world

My Neno, my grandfather's wife (Mrs. Lucha, Luisa Palestini, Luisa Raez) was a great, cheerful and enterprising woman; she raised my mother Meche, Aunt Normita and Uncle Jorge with great dedication and rigid discipline. Her mother, Mrs. Juanita, played the good cop while mi Neno played the bad cop.

I remember her from the time I saw her spinning around the living room of her house, doing physical exercises like a log rolling on the floor, in her case to keep herself beautiful and healthy. A beautiful portrait, an oil painting of her beautiful image presided over the great hall of her house on Jirón Huayna Capac. In that great portrait she looked very beautiful, elegantly dressed in a striking lilac-colored dress. Two small earrings of brilliant diamonds highlighted her smiling serenity while contrasting with the modesty of the jewelry and the beautiful bareness of her firm chest that drew one's attention; the shawl of the same transparent lilac color falling below her bare shoulders, gave her image a touch of solemn provocation; around her neck and on her bust there were no necklaces nor broaches or anything that distracted. And the mole, oh, the mole on her face, made her more beautiful and enigmatic. It was a distinguished, majestic and feminine portrait, very feminine.

The enormous painting, more than one meter twenty by eighty centimeters wide, framed in fine and elaborate cream-colored wood, with the blurred background between of white and green, made an imposing play on the also green living room furniture. The discreet cream color of the large carpet attenuated the colors. Nothing and no one moved in that house without the authorization of mi Neno, who watched you wherever you went from the large living room.

I remember her as being forever affectionate, until the last day of her life. She always had a special way with me, she would serve me stuffed avocado for lunch, she presented it in the same way she did many times to conquer Papaíto so he would marry Mamaíta. She never failed to invite me to her birthdays. She gave me my grandfather's pistol after his death, as well as my membership to the Jockey Club. When we were young university students, mi Coque, mi Tiringo the naval cadet, and I would always show up at her house the day after her birthday to greet her, eat stuffed avocado and, mainly, choose two or three bouquets of flowers each to give to the girls or have them sent with a note to my Aunt Chavalita, Aunt Viruchita or Aunt Olguita, remaining close to our dear aunts. On her birthdays, mi Neno would receive many, many, many bouquets of flowers from her friends, the wives of diplomats.

"*Tanto le piccole quanta le grandi navi... hanno bisogno del timone*," was inscribed on the small multicolored pottery, adorned with flowers in brush strokes that hung on the wall of the terrace in the house of mi Neno and my grandfather Ernesto. No doubt mi Neno, who prided herself on her Italian roots, had placed it there. I never asked her the meaning of the phrase, many times I tried to understand what it meant, I tried also to memorize it; but its correct meaning, contextualized and exemplified would not make any sense to me until many years later.

"The little as much as the big ship . . . both need a rudder," would that mean that both the big one, my grandfather, and the little one, mi Neno, needed good steering? Or perhaps the little one and the big one are the same? My brother Tiringo says that it does not refer to the helm, but to the helmsman, that is to say, to the one who steers the ship. Be that as it may, that little piece was there for every visitor or inhabitant of the house to see, obliged to see it, as the place where it was displayed, made it impossible to be ignored. The rhyme of its text and its Italian sound when read made it a singular attraction of the mansion.

A little farther on, another little piece, made of the same ceramic and ivory, read thus: "*Il tempoperso con il tempo non viene recuperato, ne il tempo viene recuperato con azioni perso.*" This small piece had a preferential place: what did it say, what did it want to tell us?

Many years later, after my grandfather's death, the house was inherited by mi Neno and her three siblings: Aunt Normita, Uncle Jorge and my mother Meche. Mi Neno, who owned 50% of the house and inherited a quarter of the other half, very generously sold the house so that my mother and my uncles could receive some money from their father's estate.

After a very difficult search, mi Neno, with the money from the part corresponding to her property, bought a house with a smaller plot of land in the district of Santiago de Surco. By then already a real estate expert, mi Neno along with sweet Delicia, her very spoiled adopted daughter, brought me to see the new property. They showed me the living room, the main dining room, and the dining area and the kitchen. On the second floor they showed me the three bedrooms and on the third floor the additional bedroom and bathroom. The house, I was told, had the same number of rooms as the original mansion, the same openness, beauty, and spaciousness. All the furniture, paintings, and other ornaments came from the original house. There they could all live, all with the same comfort, with the same happiness, although in the absence of my grandfather.

Back on the first floor, they showed me the garden, it was similar to, yet smaller than, the original; at the side of the garden, extending from the dining room was a beautifully decorated terrace with the objects of the previous house. On this terrace was the little ceramic and ivory piece, the little picture that said: "*Tanto le piccole quanto le grandi navi hanno bisgone del timone.*" From the eyes of mi Neno, the smile of Delicia, and the satisfaction of the wonderful Angelica, the girl who came from Polloc and accompanied mi Neno for many years hence, I understood that mi Neno had "the most beautiful house in the world." That is how, since that time, it is said all over the world that "things are not as they are, but as people perceive them to be." The majestic painting of mi Neno is still there, in Santiago de Surco, presiding over the living room of the most beautiful house in the world.

"Time lost over time cannot be recovered, nor can time be recovered with wasted activity."

The portrait of mi Neno would preside over the living room of the of the house on Huayna Capac and now, today in the most beautiful house in the world

La Chuña

La Chuña was the mare that my Papá Manuelito had given me. I will not tell you that I was four years old, because you will say that everything happened to me when I was four years old; in truth, I was six or seven years old, and my godfather gave me a beautiful, trotting, small and difficult to tame mare, which received the name La Chuña, – I believe that "chuña" means light sorrel or bay, because my mare Chuña had such a beautiful color. Her yellowish-white hair made her beautiful appearance stand out. But her intemperance, her impatience and her eagerness to be free stood out even more. La Chuña was indomitable. During her first years she was ridden only once, and it was by an expert horse tamer, because nobody could do anything with La Chuña. The trainer only managed to stay on her for two or three minutes, because in a single jump she bucked the rider through the air who, by sheer luck, did not crack his skull, although he was sore for more than three weeks. In spite of all this, I did not tire of taming her little by little using a lasso, after interminable minutes of running her around the paddock with the help of two or more of Polloc's farmhands along with mi Manuel, Ernes and Coque; mi Pepe only looked on, as he was so little. Only once did I ride and walk her. She carried me to Namora in an insufferable dispute of control between rider and horse, she was rough, difficult to ride and, to make matters worse, she was a trotter. The last straw for La Chuña was that she would escape from the corrals; despite the barbed wire that was there to stop her, she would slip underneath, because she was short and did not care if a barb scratched her back.

La Chuña must have had some virtue if my Papá Manuelito had given her to me, he would never have given me a present of poor quality. A few months passed and La Chuña had a foal, a beautiful jet black colt (very black from head to toe), whom I named Furia. My brothers admired him and said that I was very lucky because he was a very beautiful colt, with a smooth gait and very fast.

Furia grew up beautifully, he was the most beautiful colt of Polloc, I could only see him on vacations: in the months of July and August or in the summer from January to March. I rode my black horse followed by my dog named Ventarrón, who was also black from head to toe.

Primavera and the white donkey

My mother Meche had a mare that was very smooth in her gait, but above all she was gentle and docile to ride, her name was *Primavera*.[46] With her, all of us children learned to ride horses. Primavera was not like her children: *Invierno* and *Verano*, spirited and dangerous foals for the children.

Primavera was part of the family; her children unfortunately either died young, or perhaps were sold, or exchanged for some pig, rabbit, duck, sheep… or anything else beneficial to the house for which mi Mamaíta would skillfully use to negotiate.

Primavera was not only easy to ride, she was also easy to "*chapar*" – to be caught –, as she did not run rampant through the green pastures of the paddocks in order to avoid being caught.

Mi Papaíto had arranged the paddocks to be used by the animals in order of priority: the first to enter the resting paddocks – which were large and had fresh grass – were the milking cows, those that were giving milk, those that were "in production," of which there were about three hundred black and white, mooing, happy, beautiful and thirsty cows; the second in priority were the "dry" cows – those that did not produce milk but were pregnant, there were about a hundred and they entered the paddock when the first cows had already been moved in. After them came the horses – our horses – there were about thirty of them, no more than forty, and then, in that same paddock, the farm workers' cattle also entered. At the beginning, the fourth group put out to pasture were the sheep, but after a few years mi Papaíto banned them because they chewed the grass so close to the soil that it was almost

46 *Primavera* – Spring, Invierno – Winter, Verano – Summer

unusable. So the sheep grazed in another place, in the *Pampa de las Totoras*, a humid area full of vegetation, full of the cattails that when dried are used to make baskets.

So it was, to look from the top of the Polloc farm, from the pampa towards the edge of the Polloc river, to look at the "*abijadero*"[47] as mi Papaíto called his beautiful possession, was very beautiful: on the left, the first green paddocks, starting with those that had the short grass, followed by one or two paddocks with the medium-sized grass, then those with shiny and tall grass, then a green one, very green, with a great abundance of. If you looked at the next ones to the right, you saw the dairy cows in large pastures, white cows with black spots or black with white spots, beautiful, mooing and drinking water from the small irrigation ditches that flowed towards the river. In the next paddock, dry cows, like little live dots, more scarce, in medium sized pastures, the bellies full of the next calves to come. Next to this, in the paddock with short pastures already cut in half and eaten by the cows, the horses, oh, the horses: our horses! There, amid the short, pointy grass, and puddles of water, we had to catch them, "*chapar*" we used to say, take the horses and then just walk them around. How beautiful, nostalgic were Polloc's paddocks! The mare Primavera and the rest of the horses: La Blanca Luz; La Chuña; El Campeón (who I believe was also a son of La Primavera), mi Manuel´s beautiful colt, with his long mane, just like the other colts; La Blanquita (the mare of Joaquin Casas, the foreman of the hacienda); La Mensajera, my father's favorite mare; El Junín, the one from the early years of my parents' lives at the hacienda; the daughters of Mensajera: La Golondrina and La Perla (both huge sorrel mares like their mother; Golondrina, more reddish, similar to her mother; La Perla, more bay in

47 Pasture or Sheep pasture

color, both with beautiful white manes and lustrous skin); La Baya; La Castañita; others and at some time three or four big horses, taller and trotters, that the police left to graze.

La Primavera was the first horse I ever rode without a saddle, bareback, as my older brothers and sisters did and as my younger brothers and sisters would later ride. Mi Mamaíta rode La Primavera with great elegance and prudence, my mother's hat stood out because it was so big, the image of my mother on horseback was imposing yet sweet. The longest rides, all on horseback, were to the old mill of Chuchún (the name of my father's second hacienda to the east of Polloc), the old mill slowly shelled and broke the wheat grains, turning them into a soft flour.

My mother would bring her beloved white donkey loaded with two sacks of wheat that, when ground and turned into very fine flour, completed a single sack more than a meter high and almost as thick as a willow tree trunk. The sack, by being filled with flour, turned into a white lump that, when loaded on the back of the beloved white donkey, formed a formidable spectacle: the white donkey would stand up beautifully, raise its head, its belly bowed with the weight of the white flour, its haunches bent and one of its legs with the hock bent, and thus it would stand, against the distant horizon of green meadows and blue sky, a white statue that bewitched the eye and smit the heart. The statue of the peaceful white donkey, loaded with the white sack, competed with the most beautiful statues of *carrara*,[48] it equaled them in beauty, it surpassed them in tenderness. The content, the white flour to make bread, would later quell the hunger, and in the company of my mother, my father and my brothers would rise to God.

48 Referring the region in Italy where marble is extracted

The return home, then at five-thirty in the afternoon, was grandiose: La Primavera carried my mother at the head of the caravan, followed by a white donkey carrying its white bundle, followed by five children on horseback, tired, dusty and with the outline of their little mouths painted with white flour. In front, behind the external gate of the house, my father was waiting under the bell, and my sister Polita was running towards my mother and towards us, radiant, excited, hungry, waiting for the flour to prepare the *cachangas*[49] at six o'clock in the afternoon.

49 A baked, or more typically fried, cheese-filled pastry

La China Linda

Riding in the pampas of Polloc on my horse Furia, now tamed, was sensational, even better if it was Carnival time. I was about ten or eleven years old and I was already riding that black, elegant, triumphant horse.

The end of the Carnival festivities were being celebrated while the horses in the pampa of Polloc were walking everywhere, and the celebrators were ready to cut the *unsha*[50] tree that, loaded with fruits and gifts, would soon fall following the chants of "Chilalito chilalo:"[51]

Chilalito chilalo.
Cabecita 'e chicharrón,
a one, and a two,
and a three, machete.

And, wham! a machete blow, and if the people singing around the tree were anxious to get the presents, they might get two or three.

The unsha party was in full swing. Colorful streamers adorned the tree laden with gifts. This year the tree was bigger. The talc on the faces of the *Chinas*[52] Cajamaquiñas made them more beautiful: their reddish cheeks and big, dark, lively eyes

50 50 Unsha (pronounced "eeunsa") is the name from Quechua that is given to the tree and the party that consists of hanging gifts from the branches, after which dancers sing and dance around it, stopping for moments, and with machete blows they cut the tree until it falls in order to collect the gifts and fruits in a riotous rejoicing

51 51 "Chilalito chilalo" is part of the lyrics, and also the name, given to the traditional Cajamarca chant sung during the unsha celebratio

52 52 China, (pronounced "cheena") or chinas in plural, is the name given in Cajamarca to the native female population. China has the meaning of "chola cajamarquina," but also denotes the meaning of beautiful. Thus "Paquito and his brothers called their little sister Pola – "Mi China."

adorned the smiles on their lips cut by the dry weather and the singing in their voices. The men took the machete and tried to fell the tree. The women did the same, but they were more eager to not yet fell the tree, but to prolong the party. My brothers, undistinguishable amid the throng, holding hands in a cheerful round that spun at every note of the songs with greater speed, despite not having eaten lunch so as not to lose a minute of partying, danced, laughed and occasionally sipped half a glass of *chicha*[53] or a glass of *cañazo*.[54] I saw them. My father was not there, my Mamaíta Meche was around in one of the huts having chicken soup, boiled potatoes with *chicche*[55] and for dessert a *quesillo*[56] with honey. She preferred to eat a little, just a little, two or three dishes, before going to watch and dance the unsha.

Furia had a smooth, dancing gait, the sound of his hooves as he walked was harmonious. A good rider on a Peruvian *caballo de paso*[57] should not move in the saddle, a good *caballo de paso* does not make you feel the pounding of his hooves in his elegant, distinct, beautiful gait; I was sitting in almost perfect balance. The sound of the other horse's steps behind us confused me for an instant.

Behind me, a rider, an employee of the hacienda, majestic, was riding China Linda, a very beautiful mare, now old, shining, and imposing. China Linda was Polloc's most beautiful mare. She was not as tall as Blanca Luz, my father's favorite mare, but she was big, well-muscled, wide skeleton, strong

---

53 There are varieties of chicha, here the reference is to chicha de jora, which is a fermented corn libation

54 Cane liquor

55 *Chicche* is the *huacatay* plant (black mint, native to South America) ground and whisked, with a little salt and sometimes a few drops of lime juice. It is served as a condiment for a variety of dishes

56 An artisanal farmer's cheese, here served as a sort of flan or custard dessert

57 A particular horse bred and trained for a special smooth gait

body, dark brown with a white mane, and a fast, majestic gait. The rider approached me and said: "Little boy, I'll trade you my China Linda for your black horse." So he said to me and, seeing my surprised face, which he mistook for denial, he added "I'll up the offer and include her colt behind her." He said that and remained silent, waiting for my answer. The colt behind her was a pretty filly, almost a year old, identical to her mother, in good condition and playful.

Moments later I was riding China Linda, my hat held in my right hand, moving it back and forth from the top of my head to my forehead, elegantly back and forth, waving to the unsha dancers; my left hand tightened the reins, rounding the unsha in an outer circle. I was followed by the filly in similar gait to that of her mother. A smile of satisfaction lit up my innocent, youthful, almost baby-like face.

China Linda was very easy to ride. Fury was more hostile, irreverent, practically disobedient, more of a trotter. I will say, in favor to him, he wasn't so smooth: remembering that he was the son of La Chuña, a trotting mare, not a caballo de paso. The change was magnificent: from that day on I rode Polloc's most beautiful, most docile and well behaved mare. My brothers and my father, less knowledgeable than me in negotiation, told me that he traded her because China Linda was already old; however, a few weeks later she gave birth to another beautiful filly. A short seven years later I was riding China Linda, with the little foal at my side and the filly a few meters behind, both mine as well. Within a few years I would have more horses than my father and all the landowners in the region.

Horses fly away to heaven

I jumped out of bed, ran to the second floor window of the Polloc farmhouse, I was eleven years old, it was three in the morning, my brothers and sisters were all asleep in their little beds, my parents on the second floor. Silence, all was silence, except for the trotting, the agitated running of a thousand horses escaping from the adjoining stables. We never left the horses in the stables, we always left them in the paddocks or they returned on their own. We didn't have even a hundred horses. I jumped over the thick wall and opened the two windows. Solitude, the black sky, the noise of a thousand horses going off into infinity, into the sky. I saw nothing. The night was dark.

The city of Cajamarca was darkened that Wednesday, December 30, 1964. Already awake and ready to have breakfast, my father announced that we had to go back to the city: my Grandmother Pola had died; she was resting in peace. My trembling father picked up the phone, my mother stroked her hair, mi Manuel cried and I felt a dagger in my stomach. At three o'clock in the morning the most solemn lady in town, the matron of the family, had passed away. At three o'clock in the morning the ghost horses ran to the heavens.

I apologize for not narrating the merciless days of the wake, the weeping and the feeling of uneasiness. The pain still overwhelms me. The wake was at my grandmother's house. I will only say that I was by my mother Delish's side; I wiped her tears, I caressed her tirelessly, I suffered and cried with her. Mi Manuel did the same with my father, mi Ernes with my mother Meche, my younger siblings, confused, were dispersed to the homes of their kind aunts who lavished much love upon them. I was only separated from my mother for a few hours because I was taken, so as not to suffer, to the home of my Uncle Fermin and Aunt Evita, the parents of my Aunt Mayita Anduaga, to whom I pay homage here. My little friend Ramon Anduaga accompanied me, devotedly joining me in my grief. I will never forget him.

The unknown soldier

In the mornings the chirping of the birds woke us up very early. The melodious voices of my cousins ran over each other. The house had a halo of joy and well-being. I don't know if it was the timbres of the voices or the hint of the French language biting the letter "r" that made me confuse the voices of Marisse, Jacko and Mirelle, my loving Turpaud cousins.

In order not to abuse the kindness of my Papá Manuelito and Aunt Teresita, we went in the summer of 1965, when I was twelve years old, with my mother Delish, my mother Perpetua, mi Rafi and Alicia to stay at the house of my Uncle Alberto and the wonderful Turpaud cousins after the death of my Grandmother Pola, and later staying two weeks in La Joyita and then more than twenty days in Santa Cruz 737, where my Papá Manuelito and Aunt Teresita stayed.

My Uncle Alberto's house, European in architecture, with small roofs that fell on the sides to let the scarce drizzling rain flow, and looking beautiful and cozy, was on a very beautiful street full of leafy trees that provided shade to the sidewalks, the drive, and the house. The street was called *Soldado Desconocido* (Unknown Soldier), and there I found the shade that I longed for as a pre-adolescent from the mountains spending the summer in the hot capital.

My cousin Marisse, with her beautiful gaze, was quiet. She didn't seem to like being so beautiful. She didn't talk much and when she did, she only said sweet, simple words; never did a grave or disdainful word come out of her mouth. My cousin Jackeline (Jacko) was the second of three sisters, which was the sandwich of the house. Serene, always correct and precise in her speech, showing maturity in spite of her young age, and being her father's darling, she always let her sisters intervene first, which she still does to this day. Mirelle, quick-witted, enthusiastic and always lucid, being the youngest, demonstrated a great rapport with my mother Delish, in spite of the great difference in their ages. My cousin Michell, dashing, elegant, a haughty and alert young man, was only in the house for a few hours. My Uncle Alberto would say to him: "If you can take little time for yourself, come home."

That is how I enjoyed my cousins' friendship during that time in the house with the hardwood floors, large curtains in the dining room, and the neatness of their presence, on Soldado Desconocido Street 465 in the Santa Beatriz neighborhood. That is how I saw them that summer at my young age, just as I had seen them many years before when they arrived to Cajamarca.

In Cajamarca, my Uncle Alberto had his study on the second floor of my Grandmother Pola's house. The entrance was through a small door at Jirón Cajamarca 616. A wooden staircase took you up two flights to the second floor. You arrived at a distribution hallway that groaned with each step leading you to the wide balconies of the second floor; but, if you first turned to the left, you saw an opaque, double wooden door which my Uncle Alberto kept half-open. If, stealthily, you put your little head between the doors, you would see him sitting in front of a stately desk: dour, a few gray hairs adorning his abundant well-groomed light-brown hair with blond highlights, combed straight back. White-skinned and of Latin genotype, he smoked a pipe that he swung back and forth in his thin-lipped mouth, always looking well and carefully groomed. There was no doubt that a French gentleman of great inner nobility inhabited that slender body dressed in fine trousers.

The mother of my female cousins and cousin Michelito, my Aunt Carmelita, passed away while still young. I remember her, perhaps already ill, walking along the second floor balconies dressed in a pink gown. The color of her face was pale, her medium-length hair waved slightly and brought out her beautiful and innocent brown eyes, or maybe they were black, because they stood out in the rainy Cajamarca sunsets. I would like to say here, if you will permit me, why my father and my mother Delish did not adopt the compound Cacho-Sousa surname despite having inherited both surnames from their mother. They did not do so, as mi Julish and my Aunt and Uncle Cacho-Sousa did, in honor of my Aunt Carmelita who, being the only sister of my grandmother's father and my Papá Manuelito, did not carry the Sousa name, yet was as much a sister and as beloved by my Papá Manuelito. My mother was once heard to say: "And how would I explain this to my Turpaud cousins?"

On that second floor, from time to time, my beloved cousins would visit us in Cajamarca. The cousins' visit excited us: the second floor balcony surrounding the courtyard of the house was filled with joy. Mi Manuel, mi Érnes and I would sit at the fountain in the center of the courtyard to watch our cousins walk along the wide balcony and call them by name. If Marisse came down, we would shout from below: "Cousin Marisse! Cousin Marisse! She would just raise her hand, turn red and run past. If cousin Jacko passed by, we would call out to her: "Cousin Jacko! Cousin Jacko! Cousin Jacko would look serene. "Hello, cousins," she'd say and continue her leisurely pace. If my cousin Mirelle passed by, I don't know why we would say to her: "Cousin Betty! Cousin Betty!" She would stick her tongue out at us: it was obvious she didn't like to be called Betty. I promised that would be the last time I would call her Betty.

My cousin Michell was also there. He was the only one who would come downstairs to visit and go for walks with mi Julish. My mama Perpetua called him "niño Michelito." He would say: "Call me young Michell or Mr. Michell, Perpetuita." Whenever my cousin would come into the house, my grandmother would be put in a good mood and her generosity would increase.

She would pull out the boxes of Danish cookies that she always kept well supplied in her large wooden closet and share them with my cousin, mi Julish and us. My cousin Michell, upon entering the living room to wait for the cookies and mi Julish's frequent delay, would invariably leave a pair of fine glasses on the center table (it occurred to me that they were French-made), a key ring with more than seven keys, a silver cigarette case and a benzene lighter. Cousin Michell, Michelito, was very nice and polite, affectionate, formal and endearing. He would give my grandmother a very long hug, so long that it made me think, not that he was arriving, but that he was saying goodbye. It seemed to me that he was always saying goodbye.

My female Turpaud cousins are three angels who, by chance or by divine intention, came into this world. Their true origin must be in heaven. The Turpaud cousins never fail, they never failed my mother, and they were always there when my mother needed them, whether it was during the death of her mother, some illness, the death of mi Coque or Paquito's tooth falling out. Their presence, their empathy stand out among all human virtues.

There is no explanation to the understanding of what three angels are doing on Earth, in the same place inhabited by a saint, a hero or some unknown soldier.

The canchalucos

The *zarigüeya*, also called "rabopelado," is a marsupial mammal the size of a small dog or fox. This opossum hunts chickens at night and eats them for dinner, as well as ducks, rabbits and guinea pigs.

It has an appearance similar to that of rodents: bulging eyes, pointed snout and a long, naked prehensile tail that it uses to carry its young back and forth. It lives throughout the Americas and its name in Cajamarca is *canchaluco*. It is a nocturnal animal and eats everything, so it is said to be omnivorous.

The Plaza de Armas of Cajamarca is sloped in such a way as to allow the water that falls from the sky after the black clouds are pushed by the winds that blow from the western *jalcas*[58] to flow away. The storms leave the gardens green, the tiles clean and paint the geraniums a reddish purple. Once the sky clears and the bright sun appears surrounded by white and whimsical figures, you can see the square in all its splendor and above it, a small street that climbs flirtatiously, beckoning you to walk.

As children we called the zarigüeyas "*canchalucs*" because we had never seen the name in writing. We had never seen them up close either, only one night did we see one running across the roofs after being woken up by the noise of the chickens in the barnyard. Our mothers and Polloc's cook told us that they were monkeys that would take the chickens if we didn't keep them well guarded in their coops. My mother Meche also told us that many times some thieving employees blamed the canchaluc for the disappearance or theft of the animals from the pens.

---

58 Mountain peaks

Jirón San Martin in the city of Cajamarca is perhaps the most beautiful street in the city. It starts at the highest part of the Plaza Mayor, from its very center. The street climbs some eighty yards, adorned with flowers that look out from the windows and balconies until it reaches Jirón Junín. If you walk along the sidewalk on the left, if your lungs are agitated and your heart quickens, it is not due to altitude sickness, but because before you take a hundred steps you will find yourself in front of the house where the canchalucs lived.

As the canchalucos sleep in the upper part of the trees and stick their heads out of the holes where they live, one afternoon when I went out, in the early sixties, to the back of the house where the corral was and my mother Delish was starting to build a small structure, while playing a little drum, I saw three children with bulging eyes climbing on the house across the street and I thought it was like a tree with a burrow. Climbing over each other, they looked out from the balcony of the house. Their curious glances, their sharp eyes and the movement of their little heads seemed to me to be proof that they were canchalucos. So the children who lived there were baptized with the name of Canchalucs.

The Canchalucs: Litta, el Chino and Zarquito Balarezo Gayoso lived with their mother Doña Violeta, a sweet and very beautiful brave woman who raised five children: the three Canchalucs plus Ricardo and Emilio Cacho Gayoso, the latter two brothers of a slightly older mother. The thing is that the Canchalucs, especially Chino, were bellicose, mischievous and streetwise boys. When the Canchalucs had a dispute in the street, they resolved it with kicks; thus was born a certain rivalry and some little insults that they would hurl at my brothers and me from the balcony and that, without a doubt, were answered by us, especially by mi Coque who was an emboldened and reactive child. The greatest rivalry and dark looks were between Chino, who had a huge head, and my very skinny Ernes. Fortunately those little fights never became bigger. After a few years, a beautiful friendship grew between the two male Canchalucs and us, a friendship fostered by the one between my mother Meche and Doña Violeta, the mother of the Canchalucs.

On Monday morning, May 24, 1965, my mother Meche, pregnant for the tenth time (it was not yet known if it would be a boy or another girl), went out very early in the morning when some very tragic news shook her soul. On the little street San Martin, at the back of our big house on Jirón Cajamarca, leaving by the door of the corral, in front of it, on the second floor, her friend the sweet Doña Violeta, the mother of five children, died after a painful illness. This event hit her very hard until it caused her to give birth, which occurred the following day, May 25, when a charming little girl was born: my sister Mechita.

The three children, already orphaned by their mother, walked around our house for several weeks grieving and their tears were wiped away by my saintly mother who took care of them with great devotion while nursing and caring for her baby, helped by my Mama Perpetua.

The Canchalucs were now in our home. Mi Coque arrived home the first day singing a song that said: "*Con el saco sobre mi hombro*," carrying his brown sheepskin jacket on his shoulder, brought from the United States by my mother a few years before. He entered my mother's room to meet his new baby sister. The surprise was tremendous: not only did he find a baby sister, but also the three Canchalucs in our mother's room.

Of the three orphaned children, the youngest, the one with the shining, little dark green eyes, the most tender and playful, remained in the house as another brother. The same age as mi Pepe, with the same kindness and the same dreams, they made a fraternal friendship, almost the same but more intimate than the one all the brothers professed to him, and that he professed to us (it is worth mentioning that this brotherhood exists until today). El Zarquito, our Zarquito, mi Zarquito Balarezo Gayoso was at that time a companion of adventures, mischievousness, and joking. Even today he is a tireless joke teller.

These lines are a tribute to him, to his nobility, his good heart and his indefatigable spirit of self-improvement.

Violeta Gayoso, tireless and loving, with her five children: Ricardo and Emilio Cacho Gayoso, Litta, Chino, and Zarquito, in the late 50's. Zarquito is the youngest, dressed in white

Blanca Luz the mare

Catching Blanca Luz in the Polloc paddocks was a very difficult task, not only because she was a tall, very tall mare, but also because of her spirited and indomitable temperament. Blanca's forehead stood out in an airy look as she ran in a desperate gallop to avoid being caught. She was coming at us at full speed with her hooves spinning like a Peruvian caballo de paso blender. Seven children catching the horses at five in the morning should be enough if they knew how to handle the lassos, run through the marsh grasses and not panic when the foals and mares came at them in a frenzy, led by the difficult Blanca Luz. To catch ("chapar," we used to say) Blanca Luz was a task that lasted more than an hour; the rest of the horses that we had to ride in the morning were caught in less than ten or fifteen minutes each.

For a better understanding, we should point out that the smaller horses weighed over three hundred kilos, had their four hooves with *cascos*,[59] and natural abilities to run in the fields and paddocks of Polloc. There were six or sometimes seven children "catchers," including Zarquito Balarezo, and later there were three or four of us, after the two older ones had become teenagers. The smallest at one time was mi Pepe and at other times mi Caly, who only managed to raise his arms to scare Blanca Luz away when she haughtily came at him with her one-meter-eighty height, more than two-meters-thirty to her head, and her six hundred kilos. She detected that my Caly's no more than five or six years of age and weighing thirty kilos, would be the easiest to flank. The dogs of the house, led by Campeón, made matters worse because, instead of helping us in the arduous task, they would bark and scare the horses away, running

59 Rubber applied to the hooves

after them and chasing them through the paddock to the fences near the river where, near its majestic passage, left puddles that impeded the speed of our short, kid-size steps.

Thanks to the docile nature of Peruvian horses, Blanca Luz had a singular characteristic: she was impetuous, rebellious, running aimlessly to avoid our reaching her, but once she felt the lasso on her neck, even if her head had not entered, just by feeling it on her, this calmed her impulses, and meekly, very meekly, she allowed herself to be caught. Years later, my brother Kiko, when he was five years old, rode her with ease and even went under the legs of the animal, once she became meek and docile after letting herself be caught.

Riding her was divine, she was gentle, agile and very obedient. What was difficult for a child was to climb up on her, because her height required something to help, a wall or the cupped hands of another child as a boost.

Once the horses were caught with the ropes, we would leave some slack between the loop and the animal's neck, we would wrap the rope around the muzzle, run it under and towards the head behind the ears, lower it again to the muzzle and leave one end of the rope towards the horse's back so that, together with the other end, we would have reins that would allow us to lead the horse. There was no saddle, not even a blanket or a cloth. We would ride bareback like happy, rowdy jockeys in those beautiful, beautiful days of Polloc.

Since the task of catching the animals was somewhat difficult, and even more difficult if Blanca Luz was among them, the ingenious idea of going early in the morning before dawn occurred to us: go to the horses while they were still asleep. So we decided weeks later to gather the horses at four o'clock in the morning. Our ingenious idea did not take into account that, in order to get to the paddocks at that hour, we had to wake up at three in the morning and walk to the paddocks in the dark.

The Eclipse

The watch that his father had recently given him rang at three o'clock in the morning. The four children got up to go to the horses. Slowly, without making any noise, they went down from the second floor of the Polloc farm house, petted the dogs and with the required stealth, opened the outside gate to go to the paddocks.

Mi Pepe, Currito Raunelli, Coquito Gallardo and Zarquito Balarezo at the age of ten or eleven already knew the trick of grabbing the horses very early in the morning while they were still asleep. Catching them at three o'clock in the morning was necessary to find them lying down and be able to rope them. It was also essential to get up earlier than Paquito and his older brothers to "win" the best and most docile steeds. Currito, alerted by his new wristwatch given to him by his father, woke them up at three o'clock in the morning. That beautiful imported Edox watch was bought by his father and given to him as a birthday present.

It took them forty minutes to reach the paddock. They had to go up to the pampa, head to the pasture and down to the paddock in the dark. The horses were not only lying down, they were still asleep. It was difficult to pick out the best animals because they were nowhere to be seen. They practiced roping them in the American West style, throwing the lasso over their necks or heads, and forced them to stand up. With the horses tied to the ropes, each one pulling his own, they led them to the edge of the paddock.

Leaving some slack on the ropes on the left side of the animal's neck, the horses were ready to be ridden once the rope was looped around the muzzle and then over the head behind the ears, drawing the remaining length back to the muzzle, then bringing the tip up to the mane on the right side. This task and the previous one (leading the animals to the edge of the paddock) took an additional thirty minutes.

Getting on the horses was an easy task for the children if they led the horses to the side of a large stone, a dry mud fence with no stalks or spikes to prevent them from climbing, or near a grassy knoll or mound. From there, jumping onto the horse with an open right leg was for expert and agile riders. If you were not, you could put your belly on the back, push yourself up and then pass the leg. Horses were ridden "bareback," without saddles; ponchos or jackets were used to cushion the rider and avoid injuries to the coccyx caused by bouncing on the horse's back (the latter was serious if you did not keep pace with the horse's movements, in rhythm with its gait, and more serious if you rode for a long time).

The return home was to be triumphant, even if the sun had not yet risen. After two hours and when, according to Currito's reading, the portentous watch marked five o'clock in the morning, they arrived at the hacienda house.

The triumphant entrance was not possible because when they arrived at the farmhouse nobody saw them. They were waiting for Papaíto, Mamaíta and the children to see them arrive like American cowboys, proud, on their horses. Everything was dark, nobody was waiting for them, much less breakfast. The clock read ten minutes past five and the whole sky was black. They had no doubt: an eclipse was shadowing the Polloc ranch. They understood that it was not a partial, but a total eclipse, and they were alarmed. In increasingly louder voices: "Eclipse! Eclipse! "Eclipse, Papaíto! Eclipse, Mamaíta!" "Eclipse, brothers! Eclipse!" the children shouted in exasperation.

The announcements of "Eclipse! Eclipse!" woke everyone up. They stuck their heads out of the second floor windows.

The darkness didn't allow them to see the riders, only the screams filled the air. Papaíto came out of the second floor bedroom in his pajamas and shouted, "Go to sleep, brats, go to sleep, it's three in the morning!

According to the Zarquito, an imported watch sold by the kilogram at the Ecuadorian border, it occurred, was two hours ahead, but this is not so. The fault was Currito's eyesight. The watch is so good that he has kept it until today (2021).

Currito's original watch. He has kept it for more than fifty years

The five falcons

The Mexican movie *Los Cinco Halcones*, which we saw at the Los Andes movie theater in 1962, made a great impression on all of us siblings. Zarquito Balarezo apparently did not see it or if he did he was jealous of it and its stars Luis Aguilar, Miguel Aceves Mejía, Demetria González, Joaquín Cordero and Javier Solís.

We took the horses that morning at dawn, we bridled them very early in the morning. After breakfast, we brothers and Zarquito rode, heading for the town of La Encañada. We did this quite often: going to La Encañada was the most common ride for us. The goal was to ride the horses and get to La Encañada, this is what we always did, even though we had nothing to do there.

The ride started by taking the road that, farther on, led towards the town of Cajamarca. The first stretch was a gentle climb of four hundred meters that took us into the pampa. Climbing up from the hacienda on the gently sloping road was, this time, as always, sensational.

We spurred the horses to a trot. It was nicer and safer to run the horses on the uphill paths. We leaned our bodies forward, let go of the reins, and kicked their bellies with the heels of our leather boots, sonorously kissing the sky, urging them to run and laughing all the way. We enjoyed ourselves, we lived for reaching the top and looking down on the right hand to the river, to the green pastures, were there stood two little houses, the Virgin's well and the church of Polloc.

At the small summit we halted the horses in the gorge and in a perfect line we observed the church, the beautiful church of Polloc; we did not cross ourselves or pray: we breathed, we dreamed, we were grateful. Whenever we were there we felt it, and said nothing. We loved it, and thought nothing; our minds did not do that. We did not speak, there was just our five souls. There was no thinking, only energy, only connection and affection. Our deepest essences communed with the spirits of our dead, buried at the church. Our souls thanked God for such beauty.

We only stopped to watch two or three *cargachas*[60] and then continue our ride. From the crest, we continued along the road to the turnoff. This stretch through the pampa is the one I remember the most because arriving at La Encañada was, as always, routine, beautifully routine, but routine nonetheless. We rode along, singing the song of *Los Cinco Halcones*.

The five brothers: Ernesto, Paco, Coco, Pepe and Zarquito. We pulled the reins toward our bodies to make the horses ride with their heads held high. We held the animals' necks as high as possible and began to trot and sing: "Here are the five falcons, here are the five falcons." We would sing and then we would go on at the top of our lungs, full of emotion: "Five falcons as brothers we will fight." Then we would repeat, "Here are the five falcons, here are the five falcons." "Five falcons as brothers we will fight." That was the song. El Zarquito, who came a little further back and with a more intoned voice, continued: "Now I pee soup, now I shit peas," quickly followed by laughter and guffaws.

Once at the trail head, we turned right on our way to La Encañada. The path took on a pale hue, white due to the color of the limestone hills. On the way to the village we were accompanied by white hills on the left, green meadows on the right and the river beyond. The morning was so

60 Andean woodpecker with leaden brown plumage on its head and yellow on its body and wings which lives high in the trees or in the towers of churches and in the presence of strangers makes a lot of noise - Crazy women who laugh at anything are also called cargachas

pleasant that, as we passed by the town's soccer field (the field that my mother Delish gave to the city in homage to the Virgin of the Rosary), we took a break to brush the horses, let them eat their hay, stretch our legs and breathe the fresh air.

We arrived at La Encañada. We tied the horses at the place assigned to the mules: a hitching post at the entrance of the village, with its muddy ground, donkey and horse droppings, and a horizontal bar attached to two long stakes where we tied the reigns. We went to the small square and entered a store. We didn't buy anything at that time. There were a few times when we bought some *Pintalengua*[61] candy or a Trigoso brand soda (I preferred strawberry, my brothers, orange, Zarquito, lemon). None of were made from strawberries, oranges or lemons: the names and colors were just to distinguish one from the other).

We walked around the plaza, visited another store next to the church, which was always closed, except on Sundays when there was only one mass, which we never attended. On Sundays the campesinos would come down to exchange their products, sitting haphazardly around the gardens inside the plaza. We didn't buy anything in that store (we almost never did), we just went in to look and be tempted by the *acuñas*.[62]

After two more laps around the plaza our walk ended as it always did. We mounted our horses and we headed back to Polloc. The horses feel lighter as they return home: if you loosen the reins a little, within a few minutes they'll start running. They wanted to hurry back to graze in their paddocks, we were in the same hurry to have lunch and then in

61 Tounge paint

62 A candy made with thick cane honey and peanuts in small tubular portions, usually wrapped in cellophane paper

the afternoon to play *trinquitas* or, get on the old tractor and play like we were driving.

Scene from the film directed by Miguel M. Delgado: Los Cinco Halcones (1962)

The trinquita race

Nothing can match the passion, the enthusiasm and joy that my siblings and I put into playing the *trinquita* race. I have never lived more beautiful moments. Trinquita races with my brothers were a masterpiece of divine creation and were undoubtedly the most sublime moments that any human being could experience.

The "trinquitas" were small boats without any regulated form, whimsy or preconception. They were simply pieces of sticks that we prepared with our hands by breaking various branches, pieces of trunks any type of tree or shrub; they could also be seeds or dried fruits whether they be from orange trees or eucalyptus. In my experience, pine twigs were the best because they were faster. We made the trinquitas like quick and anxious artisans. We threw them into the crystal clear water that ran through the irrigation ditch, we chased them, and we made them so that they were faster than those of our brothers. We waited for them at the end of the course and then collected them, restoring the victorious and most exciting ones for yet another competition. What beauty, what happiness!

Describing the trinquita races is not possible without presenting the main protagonist. The race course was a very clean irrigation ditch that sprang from the well of the Virgin of the Rosary next to the church of Polloc, our beloved Polloc. It ran for more than 300 meters to the hacienda house, the race route began at the upper part of the family property. The portentous irrigation canal carried clean water, distilled by the stones and the soil upon where the Virgin Mary stood, a spring of unparalleled freshness. Drinking the water, is a rite of purification, it bathed your insides. One can't simply say that the water is delicious, even though it is. About that water, about those waters, everything can be said; it is clean, fresh, transparent, pure crystalline water, pleasing not only the palate, but good for all that every sensitive human being has inside.

At its widest, the canal was one and a half meters where it sprung from the Virgin's well reaching the uppermost part of the property, narrowing until it became a mere twenty-two centimeters wide that rushed down an incline of about twenty degrees, coursing along the left side of the house about 200 paces from where we released the trinquitas, all at the same time, head to head, without even a single millimeter of separation between us (it was not fair to give an advantage to anyone in such an important competition). We ran those 200 paces, each of us attending to his boat until we reached a ninety degree turn to the right, rounding the house. This first curve was on the side of the house where my dad's study was, which was where the canal narrowed. In an instant we were turning the corner in an uproar. Some boats got caught in the curve and could only be gingerly helped along, so the stream of water could put them back into circulation. No one cheated. We all raced happily together. A channel of 60 long steps along the front of the house was sensational in its cruelly slow pace as it beautifully and deeply flowed forth. The 60 steps almost defined the race, but there was a new curve to the left, falling much faster than the first, maybe a thirty or thirty-five degree drop. The beautiful water cascaded, and with it the trinquitas, vertiginous, majestic and unbelievably beautiful, creating a fast race. The six children, Manuel, Ernesto, Paco, Coco, Pepe and El Zarquito Balarezo; plus one young girl, my sister Polita, ran, each wanting to see their trinquita triumph, only if it hadn't gotten stuck somewhere.

That's why I must repeat: "It's certain that, in heaven, the most beautiful thing has to be the trinquita race."

A beautiful horseback ride

The original idea was to have a beautiful ride, a conversation on horseback between two friendly cousins, a number of shared illusions and family goals, perhaps common or similar, uniting them in their talks and ambitions. Thus, Papaíto and Uncle Luchito Cacho-Sousa went out joyfully on a gentle and sweet horseback ride.

Papaíto had as his best equines, Junín and Mensajera, and as his closest cousin, the owner of Polloquito, near Polloc: his cousin Luchito.

Papaíto rode his big black horse, named Junín, at a gallop. He was unruly, fearless and fast; just a nose behind was my uncle Luchito Cacho-Sousa. He was snorting more than his horse, the mare Mensajera. Junín and Mensajera were a desirable and enviable pair of horses. The black-painted male, beautiful in his nature, dug into the soil in a trot with long strides. Junín could only be ridden "up front," that is to say, with an iron bridle in his mouth, and with long, strong reins, tightly braided, and plated with silver ornaments; otherwise his amazing strength could not be controlled and, worst of all, he was a steed that was unstoppable when he trotted, galloped or ran. Mensajera, a chestnut mare with a beautiful white mane, powerful in her build with a height of more than one point seven meters, also ridden "up front," could compete without much effort with Junín with long strides, agile trotting and a desire to finish first.

The two adorable cousins, brothers I would say because of their love for each other, went horseback riding that afternoon. Like alpha males each wanted to beat the other, not in life, but in the horse race. Nose to nose, neck to neck, spurless heels stung the sweaty bellies of the animals, with sounds of "go, go!" and whimsical kisses in the air they pushed the horses' spirits and yearnings for triumph on Polloc's pampas.

A "giddy up, Junín, giddy up!" from Papaíto's mouth was twice followed with "giddy up, Mensajera; giddy up, Mensajera!" from underneath Uncle Luchito's blond mustache. A whip on Junín's rump was followed by two *chicotazos*,[63] one on each side of Mensajera's haunches. The loose reins were drawn forward, haranguing the horses, the bodies of the riders leaning forward cut through the cold afternoon wind. Two hats flew and the gallop became a race.

These competitive horsemen were lost, they were experienced riders on regular rides, but not very adept at racing or riding horses like real machos. They lost sight of the fact that the powerful necks of Junín and Mensajera, while at the trot and canter were difficult to hold, racing at full gallop they became impossible to dominate.

This is the only story that mi Papaíto told of his exploits on horseback because, after this feat, he was never seen again on the back of any animal.

My father and my uncle's ages at that time were near to that of Jesus Christ. The race of Junín and Mensajera through the green pampas would have taken place in 1955 or 1956. Mensajera's breath blew in the left ear of her contender. The horses were head to head, sidelong glances between the riders. Exhalations from the horses and snorts from the riders, the reins were too loose, the harangues, the "let's go" and the "giddy up" provoked the horses' *desboque*. Desboque means that the horses were out of control. An unbridled horse is an uncontrollable vertigo and the powerful force of Junín unbridled, the enormous strength of Mensajera, without a doubt, spelled the end for these two daring riders. The hats had already

63 A flick of the reigns

blown off, the bodies of the riders like puppets jumping on the horses, the arms tired of pulling the brakes with useless results, foreshadowed that the apocalypse was approaching. Pulling and tugging on the brakes with both arms, leaning their bodies backward did not work. The horses, the mighty horses, not only would not stop, they would charge into the wind in the reckless race.

My father prayed to the saint of the impossible, my uncle Luchito promised the Virgin of the Rosary to cut his mustache and never miss mass again. A hundred meters away was the ravine, in front of the ravine an irrigation ditch, on the side of the ditch, a quagmire. Impossible to stop the mad race and the horses' mad dash, only one alternative passed through the riders' heads: to jump. So they jumped and fell into the ditch, the mud, and dishonor.

At seven o'clock in the evening two walkers, dirty, muddy, tired, hatless and defeated by the nature of two peerless equines, returned to Polloc.

Black colt, image very much like the Junín horse. (Taken from the Internet)

Paquito rides the mare Mensajera

Heaven is being in Polloc at eleven o'clock
in the morning under the sun.

The mare named Mensajera had a reputation for being dangerous. She had already run amok several times after her romp with Junín, the black colt, and the two cousin riders left muddy in the irrigation ditch. That morning she was saddled in the yard of Polloc's farmhouse. Perhaps the foreman was going out with her or the weekly worker only mounted her in order to adorn the field and pay tribute to heaven with the beauty of that animal. It had been a long time since Papaíto had ridden Mensajera and no one in recent times had been seen doing it, at least Paquito had not seen it nor was aware of any hearsay.

Now nine or ten years old, Paquito walked towards the courtyard. His thoughts took him from the trinquitas race to Baldor's book. It was a back and forth of inclinations from the country to the city, from Cajamarca to Polloc. In his thoughts the marvelous classrooms of the Cristo Rey School competed with its melodious atmosphere and the most beautiful species of birds flying about. To see Mensajera saddled, spirited, shining and not seeing anyone else in the place was an unexpected episode and a very difficult temptation to describe, and even more difficult to control. This is why it is better that Paquito himself tells us about it in his own words.

"I saw Mensajera saddled, her two front feet at the same level, one not a millimeter in front of the other, and both rear legs slightly extended to the rear, also on the same level. Upright, slender, she looked like a statue or a supernatural creature of singular beauty. She was like a painted masterpiece, the white mane glistened and the twist of her head invited me to get on the animal. I knew she was to be feared, yet I put my foot in the stirrup and jumped on the beautiful specimen. The sorrel mare named Mensajera received me as if no weight bothered her on her broad, strong back.

Riding Mensajera, the spirited one, the one with the infamy of being indomitable was magical, divine: she was a mare with a smooth gait, docile on the reins, agile, with a sure gait. Her long strides pulled through the ground effortlessly, her statuesque figure made you feel like a general at the head of a battalion and her closeness to the sky made you believe you were a saint in ascension. The width of her body made you feel as if you were on a throne or an altar. I'll say no more. There was nothing to fear, yet much to appreciate, look at the heavens and give thanks.

Eleven o'clock in the morning in Polloc, at eleven in the morning under the sun, the morning sun on the green of Polloc, the green meadow under her hooves and the blue sky at eleven o'clock in the morning in Polloc. A miracle, magic, impossible to forget."

Image identical to that of the white maned sorrel mare Mensajera (Photo taken from the internet)

My grandfather Ernesto's tank

"Let's go shopping for Christmas presents," my grandfather Manuel said to me when I was thirteen years old. "How?" I answered astonished. "Look, you're a big boy and you should know that it's not the Baby God who gives us gifts. "It's my Mamaíta who does it," he added.

The Baby Jesus, at twelve o'clock at night, very quietly so as not to wake us up, if we had behaved well all year long, if we left our little shoes well-polished in the window of my grandmother's bedroom that overlooked Cajamarca Street, and if we put inside one of them a little piece of paper listing our wishes for presents, he would leave us the presents wrapped in paper with beautiful little bells that we would tear open the following day on Christmas. All gifts were welcome, we never had a disappointment or a complaint with the gifts from Baby Jesus: he always chose the best of what each of us had wished for.

The news that mi Mánuel brought disenchanted me. I had always preferred to believe in the gifts from Baby Jesus. We went to Comercio Street (Jirón Lima), to the variety store Cidepsa, where Mrs. Norita attended us so courteously, even though my Mamaíta was a customer who bought on credit and would not pay interest. We chose some pistols. We called them pistols, although in reality they were imitation revolvers that shot rubber bullets but couldn't kill a fly. They had a range of less than two meters, but with a little imagination they could be transformed into a nightmare for imaginary rustlers, ducks in the corral and the legs of any girl passing by on the street. Those wonderful little pistols later became the pistols of *Los Cinco Halcones*.

The three dolls that my sister Polita received that Christmas were the *Llorona*, the *Caminante* and the *Cargosa*.[64] La Llorona was a nasty little doll with blonde hair and pink colors on her face, and as soon as Polita took the little blue pacifier out of her mouth she would burst into tears; Polita's playing with La Llorona did not last more than four days. La Caminante was a very enthusiastic doll. When Polita touched a little button on her back, she would start walking and say: "Mama, give me milk." Polita understood that the doll was saying: "*Mamá, dame miel*."[65] And so she would prepare hot water with a lot of *chancaca*[66] in a little wrought iron pot and forced her to take it in teaspoons that would smear all over her face and head. It was too late when Papaíto explained to her that milk meant *leche* and not honey. The blonde head of the doll was already black and turned to mush; the subsequent milk did not succeed in calming the Caminante´s moaning, much less her ugly appearance; it only managed to spoil her even more after a few days.

The doll that we called *Cargosa* was rag doll and looked like a little baby *morena*.[67] She accompanied us for a long time. She was carried on Polita's back or in her arms everywhere, whether on a bicycle, in Polloc on the horses, or on rides down the river. The doll was such a bother, Polita couldn't protect it while playing other games with us. We had to stop playing in order to stop Polita from crying, who thought that the doll could die from being thrown about. As a way of soothing the doll, Polita would take it to bed to sleep with her, as well as to breakfast and lunch. This is how the blessed doll earned the nickname "*Cargosa*." The sad end of Cargosa came one afternoon at the river in Polloc when, placed in a little wooden

64 Crybaby, Toddler, and Burden.

65 "Mama, give me honey"

66 Unrefined sugar

67 Dark skinned girl or woman

boat, went for a ride to Chuchún, Papaíto's hacienda downriver, which we seldom visited because it was so far away that it was, for us, only a place to dream about.

After a short seven days there were no more little pistols or dolls. Many other games remained to be played: trinquitas, leap frog, the robe game or five corners, if not riding bicycles, then freeze tag or hide and seek.

The constant playing of games was broken by the arrival of the parcel sent by my grandfather Ernesto. My brothers received wagons, pistols, machine guns and even a ping pong game; my sister Polita received a dollhouse with little tables, furniture and tea cups. My grandfather Ernesto, in a very appropriate gesture of affection and preference, sent me a war tank, a metal toy that worked with batteries; it had a soldier at the top who, while the tank advanced, moved an arm that hit against the metal sounding every half second "tac, tac, tac." The tank had the ability to turn around if it hit an obstacle or if you put your foot, a stone or a shoe in front of it.

My war tank accompanied me for a long time. I took it out it out to play off and on for several years. Every time I think of my grandfather, I remember the little tank that would go "tac, tac, tac," and went round and round. I kept it in my bedroom closet next to my battery-powered piggy truck that went "oink, oink, oink."

The piggies go "oink, oink"

Neither Paquito nor I remember who gave it or how it appeared at Christmas, whether it arrived with Baby Jesus' gifts, Grandpa Ernesto's gifts, or if it was a gift from someone else. It fell into Paquito's hands like a December or Wise Men's Day miracle.

It was a beautiful little toy truck. The driver, a little pig in a farm hat with a blue-ribbon around the brim. would occasionally stick his head out and turn around to look at the load behind him. Just like the little war tank, it was battery operated, it would go forward and, simply by touching an obstacle, would go backwards, turn the wheels and continue going forward again. The nicest thing about this little toy was that it carried a load of six or seven little pigs in the back that would stick their little heads out and go "Oink, oink, oink."

Gentleman and children of *fina estampa*

We left very early so we could have the first turn. We loved going to the Inca Baths. We loved to bathe and splash around in the thermal waters of the Inca Baths. That morning we would go to bathe with my mama Perpetua and it would be in the very same well where the Inca bathed, the Inca Atahualpa who, according to some historians was called Atabalipa, yet who in reality was called Ataw Wallpa (Powerful Chosen One, as translated from Quechua) and who betrayed his brother the true Inca who descended from the Cusquenian lineage, not from Quito like Ataw Wallpa. For the people of Cajamarca, the true and last Inca was Atahualpa, and he bathed in that same well and it was very enjoyable to bathe there and that was the only important thing.

We had to be nice and clean because that Saturday my Uncle Jaimito, who was an ambassador and was always very well turned-out, was visiting from Lima and he would come with my cousins Jaimito and Manolo, and the cousins as well, were always clean and formal and did not say bad words and did not have spoiled friends like our friend Shotoco Arce.

The twin-engine landed at the airport and we saw it in the distance from the door of our house. My parents went to Papá Manuelito's house, but at twelve o'clock noon the visitors would be arriving at our house. How elegant my cousins were! In fact, their little blue pants and neatly pressed white shirts looked great covering their slender bodies and narrow waists, neither too loose nor too tight, with the leather belts, not like our leather straps that, in order to hold up our pants, had to be tightened until a sort of tail was hanging down the front.

We went out with the cousins to the door of the house to look at the landscape to the south and the Plaza de Armas that beckoned us to walk, to the north the mountains, and the white clouds that presaged sun all morning and clouds in the afternoon. The conversation was about bulls, horses and riding. There was no talk of pretty girls or evening soirees; we all behaved quite formally, until Shotoco Arce arrived, and when he saw our formal cousins, he challenged them to a spitting contest, aiming at the stones left by the rains on the street or the iron railings of the windows of our neighbor Julito Martas' house. We were ashamed to have such an insolent friend, and to have him propose activities of such bad taste to our distinguished and beloved visitors. The cultured behavior of our cousins was exemplary. Manolito, with a cadenced and firm voice, told him: "Your invitation is not up to my level," and took the three steps needed to enter the house, to where Jaimito pulled him by the shirt, pushed him by the chest and made a rude gesture that left us perplexed. We entered the house and slammed the door shut. Mi Mánuel and mi Érnes were red in the cheeks, I was embarrassed, and mi Coque, as if it were nothing, felt like just another Spaniard. He walked with slow steps and told them: "Don't pay attention cousins, that dolt is beneath us."

That evening we children did not attend the big welcome dinner; my parents, Delishita and Julish gave a reception for Uncle Jaimito and Aunt Sonita in the upper part of Uncle Paquito's house. The party went on until twelve at night or one in the morning, I don't know the exact time because I fell asleep in the bedroom on the second floor from where we siblings listened to the hubbub. Our cousins slept at Papá Manuelito's house. The melodic voices singing *valses* [68]and *marineras* combined with sounds of guitars and the

68 A particular style of romantic Peruvian folk music in waltz-time

rhythm of the *cajones criollos*[69] did not let us fall sleep until a bit later. The powerful, enthusiastic and magnificent voice of Aunt Olguita stood out among all the others. Aunt Olguita's powerful, enthusiastic and magnificent voice stood out among them all. I heard three singers arrive, with guitar, *bandolina*[70] and cajon. I heard my mother Delish say out loud that this song was dedicated to Uncle Jaimito. I even heard her sing it the next day. She said it was very well deserved and that she sung it for him, very well deserved, it was the beautiful waltz *Fina Estampa*.[71] This song contains the appropriate lyrics saying: "Caballero, caballero de fina estampa."

Jaime Cacho-Sousa Castro, "Uncle Jaimito A refined gentleman

69 Creole cajones – percussion instrument mentioned in the chapter "Some jewels to fall in love with"

70 Stringed instrument, sort of a cross between a guitar and a mandolin

71 An expression meaning refined, of high quality

My abuelita Rosa

Like a gypsy sitting on an uncomfortable chair that wobbled from time to time, on a table covered with green flannel, my Grandmother Rosa would read the cards to my cousin Genio, divining her pending future.

If my Grandmother Rosa was in good spirits and had a satisfied stomach, she would sit in that chair in front of that table in my Uncle Jorge's house immersed in hope. The cousins and my siblings as well would line up to hear if Don Futuro would bring them anguish, anger and poverty or, if more generous, reward them with money, fame and a great love.

So famous did my *abuelita* become in this weaving of fates that within weeks many young people were lining up outside the door.

Her great-grandchildren, years later, would see her always smiling, usually quiet, with her shining black eyes, casting her cards on the green flannel-covered table. She was full-figured, almost always in her robe over her pajamas, with very little to say. Her face was reminiscent of Mamaíta's. Playing the lottery every week of her long life, winning the jackpot was her only illusion, as it was years before, waiting for the allowance that my grandfather Ernesto, who never left her helpless, would always send her.

She lived her last years in Huacho, next to Papaíto and Mamaíta's house in another little house with two bedrooms, a living/dining room, a bathroom, a kitchen and a small patio where she went outside to sunbathe.

The best gifts she could receive, if it wasn't some cash, were not dresses, jewelry nor shoes: she was happiest when she received something delicious to eat. I remember bringing her a Huachano breakfast consisting of tamale, half a kilo of chicarrones and two warm loaves of bread that she gobbled up in a jiffy.

Ever since then, I've always been invoked to repeat such a feast every week or during family visits.

Dogs and pigs

It is well known to everyone that the dog is man's best friend. The ones we had in my house were many. The first two were bought by my father in order to accompany him during his early days as a landowner. My father gave up his career as a sailor and went to Cajamarca in the final months of 1953. His first two dogs, a male and a female, were named *Crucero* and *Fragata*.[72] It was evident that his love for the Navy was still present; it always was.

Crucero was a huge dog, very beautiful, haughty and imposing; he had black spots on his very white velvet coat. His companion Fragata was also very refined and beautiful: her harlequin Great Dane coloring leaning towards a light lead color made her look more feminine. The joyful, tail wagging greetings of Crucero or Fragata would knock my two older brothers to the ground. The breed and size of the dogs denoted a desire to show off nobility and power. The eagerness and pride were augmented by the breeding and arrival of *Corveta*, my Ernes' dog, who was of the same color, but with more numerous and smaller spots. Later on, her little brother named *Submarino* was born. He was a slim, lanky, lead-colored spotted dog with a mysterious look. He had a half-brown / half-blue eye that matched the other eye of the same colors, but reversed.

The two giants, who induced fear into any visitor, were Papaíto's pride and joy. Both they and their daughters had one blue eye and the other leaden. They were like effigies as they sat gazing toward the horizon and guarding the house, commanding such respect and admiration that even the angels were frightened. Their sparse, hoarse barking, echoed from

72 Cruiser and Frigate

the beautiful surrounding hills. Another symphonic creature, *Violeta*, fluttered around the kitchen, a little black and white small-breed dog – woolly, straight-haired, with semi-upright ears, who was Mamaíta's spoiled little baby. My dog *Terzan* was Violeta's offfspring and brother of *Multiplication*, mi Érnes' dog, who accompanied us for many years. *Legrân*, a brave, tawny dog, was also Papaíto's pet. All of them were our first dogs in Polloc.

Black and white Harlequin Great Dane identical to Crucero (photo taken from the internet)

Female Harlequin Great Dane identical to Fragata (photo taken from the internet)

We were very young at that time. I remember the images and the tails of Crucero and Fragata. I had fun with Multiplication's antics, I mourned the loss of Terzan when the *canchaluc* took him away, I remember the jumping in the irrigation ditch, the fights with foreign dogs that Legrán engaged in and, especially, the tremendous leaps of Campeón over the high barbed wire and the sticks and stones which he brought back for no other reason than to play with the children and melt their hearts.

When the sun greeted the new day and the white cotton mounds formed figures of gods in the all-seeing and all-covering blue, we went for a ride to the pampas of Polloc. We went on horseback followed by Campeón, the new German Shepherd cross bragged about by Papaíto; we were also followed by Tina and Baby, the beautiful fine mother and daughter German Shepherd dogs given to us by my Uncle Rafael Gómez Sánchez; Jet, a younger and not so fine dog also given to us by my uncle Rafo; Ventarrón and Cien Soles, two Danish cross dogs, were also on the expedition. We loved to watch the dogs chase the pigs who invaded the fields and the piles of harvested barley. The hogs always ran away from the dogs' snapping and stopped damaging my father's paddocks and crops.

This time it was a drove of pigs, led by a huge hog with long tusks that invaded the paddock. At our voice of "sic 'em, sic 'em," the dogs ran to confront the pigs. To our great surprise, the leader, the enormous lead-colored hog, confronted the dogs with determination, followed by three or four other males. The drove consisted of more than a dozen pigs, both hogs and sows, and the surprise for us was tremendous, but it was even greater for the dogs. The pigs did not run away: they confronted the dogs with bites that the dogs happily avoided, although their tusks scratched and wounded the dogs' legs and backs.

The battle was tremendous and in order to avoid further damage we opted to retreat in the hope that the dogs would follow us and thus end the bloody throws that could prove to be fatal. When we were more than a hundred yards away, the dogs began to follow us, pursued by the hogs, the big boss in the lead and behind him the whole drove of enraged pigs. Due to my tender age, I asked my brothers not to resort to whipping the dogs in order to drive them away from the insolent enemies, but the sensible action on the part of Mánuel prevented further fighting and grief.

The walnut tree

That morning at my house there would be no boat races nor time to ride the horses; the children and my mother went out to the garden very early to pick the strawberries that were already coming out in heaps, sweet and delicious. Under the branches, we picked them in little baskets and then we took them to fill a large basket. There were also artichoke plants, those small and fleshy mountain artichokes, the ones with pointy spines that, once boiled and cooked in lemon, salt and vinegar, were very tasty. They were nutritious, had a lot of iron and made your blood red so that it would heal the wounds in case you fell off a horse or tripped over the stones when jumping over a puddle or irrigation ditch, where the sharp rocks hurt naughty little children who do not take care of themselves as mother asked.

Mamaíta's vegetable garden was large: there were strawberries, artichokes, as well as corn that we ate raw, plucked from the cornfields that turned from green to yellow as they ripened. In the corner, near the gate, in a magnificent place, lived the prince of the place; it had been there for more than two hundred years, yet it continued to look luxuriant and imperial; it was a huge leafy tree with a thick trunk and enormous branches that rose more than fifteen meters: it was the giant of the orchard, the king of that place.

The walnut tree shaded the strawberries from six in the morning until noon. In the afternoons it let them bask in the sun and gave shade to the artichokes that were then thirsty and took a rest from the sun in order to grow. A canal of clean water surrounded the orchard, watered the gardens and the plants, and further down it spilled into the Polloc River which waited for its waters that then, many leagues farther on, fed the "golden snake:" the great Marañón River.

My mother's vegetable garden, with its roses, violets and flowers of all colors, was a wonderful place. It was even more beautiful when the strawberries came out to turn its expanse red and green. My mother's orchard was a dreamy place and her most unique possession. They had a natural symbiosis: my mother's green eyes lit up when she arrived. There she felt like the owner and landlady. My mother's orchard reflected her personality, simple and impetuous, pragmatic and beautiful, close and distant, hardworking and elegant, sweet and loving, upright and unwavering. Incredibly beautiful, from any point of view.

The Walnut tree was full of fruit before the November rains began. On the outside, the fruits were green shelled balls that gradually turned yellowish or brownish. In the center, stubborn nuts refused to crack unless you hit them hard with two stones until you got to the heart; between the green shell and the walnut heart there was a thick black pasty liquid that turned your hands black, it looked like a sticky shiny tar. "Don't eat the nuts," my mother would tell us, because she was going to bake a walnut cake.

We disobeyed our mother and ate a lot of them. When we arrived for breakfast my mother asked us where we had been and if we had been eating the strawberries or walnuts. We didn't say anything, but my mother discovered the little hands of my younger brothers Pepe and Polita, blackened by the walnut tree tar.

Years later we realized that it was not the walnuts that my mother valued and watched over the most: it was the black paste that made her hair soft, shiny and black. She protected her garden from the intrusion and rapaciousness of the children: she protected the black walnut paste because it made her dark hair beautiful and soft. The miraculous black walnut paste was what my mother valued the most.

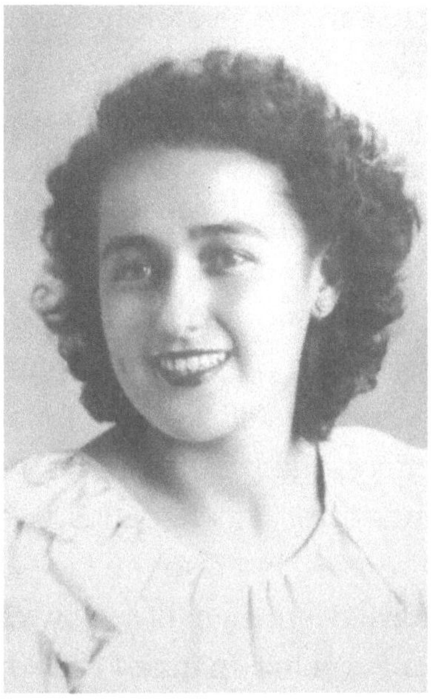

Mamaíta had to take care fof her beautiful dark hair

Paquito's hepatitis

Dr. Julio de la Puente arrived at three o'clock in the afternoon. He rushed in with his old, brown, wrinkled doctor's bag. The stethoscope detected an accelerated heartbeat. It was not necessary to use the mercury thermometer, as the fever was evident. The yellow color of his eyes, the fatigue, lack of appetite, abdominal pain, and yellowish urine facilitated the diagnosis: lying on the first floor on a stretcher, Paquito was suffering from hepatitis.

This is not some tale, nor narrated story. It intends to be a tribute, an expression and a memory of gratitude, recognition of the care, diligence and selflessness of Mamita Perpetua.

Without fear of contagion, suffering more than the patient, she provided all her care. This hepatitis was one of the most severe. Not only the eyes, but also the face and body of three-year-old Paquito turned a malignant yellow color. Even the bed sheets that Mamita Perpetua changed daily had an amber color. The prognosis was serious, a diet free of fatty foods, rum compresses on the forehead and lemonade on the lips were repeated for more than twenty days.

"It was not the care that I value most, it was her sweet company, the hours she spent by my side. I am not saying that other hands, those of my other two mothers and my father were absent, I am saying that her constant company by my side brought me out of that agony."

Antuán, the spoiled child

Paquito was quite spoiled by his mamita Delish. This particularity worried all the older members of the family. Excessively spoiling a child, they thought and said, could be harmful, as it was with Antuán. Due to so much spoiling, Paquito was nicknamed Antuán. This nickname was also given to Julish, who was also very spoiled, and I think it was given to him because of the jealousy he felt when he saw that his mother, Pola, also spoiled Paquito quite a bit. "Antuán," they said, "was very spoiled, and we should make sure that Paquito will not be an Antuán."

Nobody remembers who Antuán was anymore, only his name remained engraved in Paquito's mind. His Papaíto, if he saw him with a new present given to him by his Delishita, would call him Antuán. If he asked for something extraordinary, his uncles would call him Antuán. Antuán up and Antuán down. "This child is going to be like Antuán," they all said.

His little mother Delish just laughed. On the contrary, it seemed that these criticisms and warnings encouraged her to spoil Paquito even more. Paquito began to worry (at just under five years of age, he felt responsible for his future). He decided to ask everyone who Antuán was or had been, and what happened to him to cause so much fear in his parents and family. He never found out who Antuán was. After a long time, only once did he hear his mother speak of Antuán. Delishita told him: "I hope you end up like Antuán. Today he is a great man, very good and very prosperous," and added: "Being conceited is good. Spoiled children value themselves. They value themselves and end up well.

Julish, Julio Sáenz Cacho-Sousa, he was also spoiled during his childhood like Antuán

Felice di stare lassù

The marriage of Uncle Paquito and Aunt Mayita was celebrated in Polloc, it was an event "*de polendas*,"[73] magnificent, elegant and of great significance: the most beautiful woman of Cajamarca was marrying the man with the brightest future (and the most handsome too).

The most beautiful in Cajamarca, Mayita Anduaga, accepts her engagement to a very handsome man, Francisco Sáenz Cacho in 1960

It was on March 19, 1961. An agitated morning left pajamas, boots, shoes and dresses of all kinds on the floors of the bedrooms and even in the living room of the house. It was a complete revolution. Breakfast was eaten standing and in a hurry. My parents adorned themselves: my father's gray suit and my mother's elegant black dress. My mother Delish wore a demure dark gray dress with huge pleats at the neck that

73 Marvelous

looked like two fans. My older cousins wore suits imported from England and elsewhere, France and Portugal of course. In mi Julish's case, in order to impress the Anduaga sisters-in-law, especially Susy, she wore a silver handkerchief to match the tie; highlighting the beauty and modern charm of her blue outfit brought from Italy. The guests arrived directly to the church by car, located two hundred meters from the hacienda where we all had awakened so agitatedly.

During the moments before the ceremony, the most striking and touching thing was to see my grandmother Pola, the first to be ready: covered with a long and elegant black *mantilla*, the transparency of which revealed the shiny silver threads of hair on her little head. Her unperturbed face awaited the walk to the church and the subsequent Catholic ceremony. She was dressed in ebony, with which she would prove to be the mother, the godmother and the tree that would be the arbor for this marriage of plentitude and love.

It cannot be said what turned out to be the most spectacular: Some say the religious ceremony officiated by the Reverend Nemesio Rivera Meza, Bishop of Cajamarca, and the loving Father Serafin, a friend of the family; others say the singing, the choir and the violins; others say the beauty of the bride; cousins and guests say the elegance of the groom in tails and his smile thrown to the wind. For Paquito, the greatest thing was the walk from the church to the hacienda house.

After the ceremony, now outside the church, amidst applause and cheers, the couple set out on their more than than 200 meter walk across the grounds, including some puddles and dust, towards the hacienda house. The bride and groom at the front; further back, the godparents; my grandmother Pola and Don Fermín - Aunt Mayita's father; a few steps behind, Doña Evita - the bride's mother; the sisters-in-law; Gordo, Fermín, Ramoncito Aduaga and his little brother Lucho, who were the only ones wearing shorts and "*michi*"[74] ties. Three meters behind, the entire Sáenz family: parents, uncles and children. The distance between the groups was sufficient for everyone to be able shine in this lavish procession. A crowd of employees and campesinos of the hacienda, all along the route, applauded and cheered with their hats held high, waving them in a call to the angels, preventing them from closing in on the sky and bringing rain; the rays of other gods fell at an angle that kept the shadows from falling on the procession.

The guests joined the procession behind the main group, keeping more than three meters between each other, two violins, five guitars and a children's choir accompanied the measured steps of the participants. Next came the Cacho-Sousa family, presided by Uncle Panchito and Aunt Sarita, who were surrounded by their cousins Chicana, Marta, daughter Sarita and Alfredo (nicknamed cousin Borolas). The Rodriguez family completed the entourage: in the middle was Uncle Leopoldito surrounded by his whole family; a few steps back, Uncle Carlitos, Aunt Toya and my cousins; to the right, Uncle Victor, Aunt Carlotita, Chelita and Paquito Rodriguez Bueso de Manzanedo; then, in front of the children's choir and the violins, Aunt Tulita Rodriguez, very elegant and making an effort not to fall too far behind. She was skirting the stones and sinking her high-heels into the ground. Her round and affable face, her demeanor and her graceful walk provided the grandest touch to the procession.

While the sun shined upon beautiful spectical, the eucalyptus trees moved, dancing in the wind. The channel of sweet and transparent water, just "*ahicito*,"[75] alongside the beautiful path of stones, earth and mud accompanying the murmured

---

74 Bow ties

75 Nearby

prayers and songs. This was the most sublime and beautiful moment in that morning of sun, love and emotion.

Then later, in the house dancing, oh the dancing! First the Blue Danube. I couldn't see anything, or if I did see, I can't recall, I only heard the music. The guests in the great room crowded around the couple blocking my view with their anxious, excited bodies. Ever since that day, whenever I listen to Strauss, my eyes fill with watery liquid that emerges in tiny droplets, sliding down my cheekbones, sometimes reaching my mouth, afflicted and salty. But I don't know why they come, and I don't know why their sad joy twists my belly.

Then there were ballads, rounds, laughter. I am left alone (because the cousins were too old for me, I was only eight years old and didn't know how to dance), so it was left for me to watch, to gather memories, and from time to time, like my little brothers, grab our faithful dog Campeón for a dance on his two little hind paws to Charles Aznavour's songs and sing with Domenico Modugno: "*Volare, oh, oh... Cantare, oh, oh, oh, oh. Nel blu. Dipinto de blu, felice de stare lassù.*"

Uncle Paquito and Aunt Mayita supported by two archangels: Fermín Anduaga and Polita Cacho-Sousa

A miraculous kiss

All the children, their parents, Uncle Paquito and Aunt Mayita hovered in the yard in front of the huge "*pajero*" the place to keep the straw left over from the barley harvest, and that was used to make bedding for the cattle in the stables. The children were playing, shouting and laughing. Only two were not there: Paquico, the months-old baby, the aunt and uncle's firstborn, who slept most of the day, and little Paquito. A fever was keeping Paquito in bed. The attentions of his mother Mechita, extremely caring, made a place for a little bed very close to him in the little room adjoining her bedroom in Polloc. From there, on the second floor of the house, even the footsteps of the children could be heard through the window. Paquito could not get up, he didn't even dare to peer through the window because of the fever "that soared," so strong and abusive, preventing him from setting foot on the long and creaking floor boards that covered and sheltered the place.

To be in Polloc with all his siblings was wonderful, a dream, a pleasure that could not be lost, could not be wasted. The episode must have been important, otherwise neither Uncle Paquito nor Aunt Mayita would have been there. On the other hand, it was likely an outbreak of measles or something unknown, which worried his mother and little Paquito even more.

Late in the afternoon, his mother's sweet voice and her loving hand on his forehead woke him up: "He still has a fever," said his Mother Mechita. "He's boiling with fever," she added. "Leave him to me," said Aunt Mayita. "I'll see if he has a fever," she added as she put her lips on Paquito's forehead to measure the temperature of his little body, which was melting from so much heat. Half asleep, Paquito felt two lips on his forehead, a sweet balm calmed his spirits and his discomfort; soon after, like a miraculous lightning strike, he felt very well.

At five o'clock in the afternoon the blue sky and the white clouds slowly lit everywhere from the hills to the river. The children were drinking huge cups of milk with Milo at the kitchen table. In no less than fifteen minutes after the kiss on the forehead, they heard the calls of Paquito, coming from way out in the orchard, more than a hundred meters from the house. All the children and the two mothers ran out there. Jubilant and recovered, Paquito, perched high up in the walnut tree, shouted, "Come on and play, brothers, let's play!"

Let me cry

Under the spell of some pernicious fairy or by the divine design that sometimes is provided, and sometimes removed, the melody that is heard and is transfered to the voice is an impossible act for my whole family. We can just barely intone the national anthem. The C is elusive and even worse the D sharp. It is not a question of voice, the matter is tremendously complicated and impossible to correct. Capable of enjoying music and its charms, we find it impossible to translate a melody or a single rhythm from brain to throat. If a member of the family sings, the harmony disappears and it is possible to awaken, if not the listener's torture, the guffaws or finger to the lips indicating, politely: "It is better that you remain mute or silent," not to say: "Shut up, you little goat."

Near Mother's Day, following the instructions of teachers and my mother Delish, and without Papaíto's permission, who knew our limitations, we prepared with my siblings a theatrical performance dedicated to Mamaíta, seeing that our main interest was the games, to which we dedicated a lot of time, and not wanting to take away almost every space, remembering that each of us would dedicate a song to our mother, since learning a poem by heart would be a very difficult task.

From the first number, Manuel (my ten year old older brother) ran off. Mi Mánuel hated it when I foisted any acting, singing or poetry upon him. He never learned a poem, let alone wanted to recite one. It was possible that precisely because of his shyness he had never learned a poem, a phrase or a harangue, for fear of having to say them in public.

Tiringo was secretly preparing his number and as he was not quite ready, he gave me his turn. I had not prepared myself and when I went to the stage I could only think of singing a song that the radio and mi Mánuel's record player kept repeating: "Es un balazo" (It's a bullet) was the name of the song. The lyrics said that this bullet "clouded my reason" and so it was. My interpretation was horrible but Mamaíta loved it, or at least that's what she said.

Then mi Coque came in to sing. He had chosen a song: "Doce Cascabeles." He thought he was Joselito, he was sure that he was identical to him and that he even had his voice. His interpretation was bad; it is not possible for a Sáenz Ráez to sing well. Mamaíta was close to shedding tears, not of emotion, but of fright: after the bullet fired, the twelve bells rang, but in the ear...

Pepiancito, dressed in tight beige overalls with short legs, was small so he was exonerated from performing, so Tiringo had no one to give his turn to. Mi Chini, the princess of the house, still a little girl, with each intervention could only hug her doll nicknamed Cargosa and cover her ears.

Tiringo's intervention, which had been rehearsed many times, started off beautifully, a lively, in tune and wonderful voice rose to the chords of the song "*Madrecita Linda, Yo Te Cantaré.*"[76] The audience was mute. Tiringo continued "Madrecita Linda, *no llore tú*;"[77] we all remained silent and attentive until the first out of tune note that could make a rooster jump. We started to laugh, but we tried to hide it, the laughter came out between our teeth. Mamaíta, touched, only looked into Tiringo's eyes. At the second rooster crow the laughter continued, while Tiringo was singing and saying: "Let me cry and don't you cry," when at once he started to cry. He began to cry. It is worth saying that he never sang again. None of us has performed in public ever since.

76 Mother Dear, I Will Sing to You

77 ...don't you cry

The Pichuchur

The ranch employees closed the stables and corrals at five o'clock in the afternoon. They had been doing so for fifteen days. If before they had tied the doors with old ropes at 6:30 p.m., these two weeks they were doing it at 5:00 p.m. with hasps and padlocks. The farm workers were frightened. My Mamaita was urging us to close the duck and rabbit pens. The matter became even more worrying when my father ordered the hacienda foreman to have the farm workers take post watchouts twenty-four hours a day. It was announced that the Pichuchur was near.

The first news came from Namora, in La Perla, Aunt Olguita's beautiful ranch, from where two sheep had disappeared. In La Quispe where my cousin Mañuco took care of, among other animals, the two most beautiful Peruvian caballo de paso colts in the whole region, three purebred steers were missing from the week's count. La. Quispe was close to Polloc. Just by crossing the Polloc River, along its banks, the pampas of La Quispe were beautifully tranquil. The Polloc's lands ran along the other bank as far as Chuchún; those of La Quispe ran parallel to the other side of the river as far as Polloquito. It was frightening, the Pichuchur was near.

He was not alone. To be able take so many cattle, he had to be heartless. In La Perla and La Quispe you could find traces in the mud of the animals that in some cases, if they resisted to be herded, after being whipped on their legs and stomachs, should they not obey their new master and his henchmen, they were dragged belly up.

El Pichuchur was a cattle rustler, a cattle thief. His business was the theft of horses and cattle. Only as a hobby would he take donkeys or pigs and when he was hungry he would also take guinea pigs, ducks, chickens and rabbits. At Easter, Christmas or if he got a new girlfriend, he would take the sheep. There were also known cases in which he took a girl. This is why the girls of Polloc were frightened, although it is said that once an ugly and a fickle lass went out at night when Pichuchur announced he would be nearby.

Tall, thin and with a pointed nose. A sparse, black beard with silver threads revealed his experience in his work. Boots, one black and the other dark brown, both knee-high, and a wide white hat that shielded his face from the sun and the stares characterized the soullessness of the now famous Pichuchur. It was said that he came from far away. It was certain that he came from Porcón, since a machete on his back and two pistols in his belt made his ferocious origin known.

Pichuchur loved the granaries. Not only did he enjoy stealing cattle, he also stole from the barley silos, made off with the alfalfa and took potatoes by the sackful. The barley, it is said, was sucked through a tube that he introduced through a hole that he made in the roofs and barns.

It was strange to know that he had robbed in La Quispe. It was well known that my Papá Manuelito respected him since he got him out of prison more than once. The latter was heard from the mouth of the black Amadeo, Manuelito's *protégé* and a wise connoisseur of hacienda traditions.

Happily, he never stole anything in Polloc. The alarm of his arrival or proximity closed the corrals and filled mi Papaíto with courage who, armed with his 22 caliber pistol, was waiting, determined for a face to face confrontation with this famous and ruthless villain of the region.

Tawa, the human gazelle

We loved to have mi Mánuel read us comics: all the children around him, looking at the figures and listening to his intoned voice. We sat on the green-painted wooden bench in the backyard of the house.

A supersonic spacecraft crashed in the forests of planet Earth. The crew, a couple from an elevated civilization were stranded in the middle of the jungle; it was impossible to repair the ship and they would have to live there for a long time in that strange, distant and splendorous place. A few months after being in that inhospitable region, their child was born, a boy they named Tawa. But a violent explosion in the crater of Naclov left both parents lifeless and Tawa defenseless. A loving black gazelle took pity on him and nursed him, raised him and taught him the language of the animals... Do you know what Naclov is? Can you read it backwards?

To survive in the jungle you had to be fast on the run, violent in the attack, and strong like the gorilla; Tawa learned this by living with the animals, speaking their language and developing instinctive skills of survival and justice.

Tawa was raised by the gazelles, assimilated the language of the animals and developed extraordinary strength and intelligence. Fortunately he meets Paty, a girl also lost from another expedition, who becomes his faithful companion and together they procreate Tawita, a boy with the same abilities as his father. Together Tawa, Paty and Tawita experience intense emotions in infernal fires, enemy attacks and a thousand vicissitudes. They are able to win a thousand and one battles thanks to the help of their friend the baby-faced giant named Etreuf and the invaluable collaboration of his flying horse, his friend Homcabagui, who displays courage, timeliness in relief and wisdom in the strategy of defense and attack upon the powerful enemies of animals, jungle and ecology...

What do you think Etreuf was like? Do you think Etreuf was a weak individual? Can you read his name backwards? Where do you think the name Homcabagui comes from?

It was fascinating to listen to mi Mánuel read the comics. We all wanted to be Tawa, Tawita or Paty. The stories lived on in our games in the vines and bushes by the Polloc River. The real enemy was Rosell, the keeper of Joaquín Casas, a haughty, bullying boy, there were no bosses or farm boys superior to him. Rosell wore a ring in the shape of a fox on the middle finger of his right hand with which, with a tightly clenched fist, he had not only knocked out several peasant children, but had cut their cheekbone or cheek, and in other cases had split their lip and left them missing a tooth. Only Tawa could stand up to him. For that, one would have to be brave and powerful as was mi Coque who, after a violent and furtive attack by Rosell while we were pretending to fly through the air from one hanging vine to the next under the *poro*[78] trees, was the only brother who dared to face him with his fists.

The enemy had followed us secretly into the bush, crossed the wide ditch without jumping over it, to intimidate us he put his feet in it, raised both fists high and told us: "What are you doing here, dammit?" He continued: "I'm going to kick the shit out of you" and rubbed the fox ring that we saw glistening on his finger. Mi Tiringo became livid and I, I admit it, did not run away because I had the bushes behind me and my legs were shaking. There was no turning back, my heart was pounding, "What to do?" I asked myself as I resigned myself to a beating. Suddenly mi Coque shouted: "I am Tawa" and jumped from the top of the poro tree. Rosell was bigger, we all feared him, but that time mi Coque appeared undaunted. He gave a second shout: "Homcabagui, come to me" and hanging from a poro tree he jumped to the

78 A fruit native to the region

edge of the ditch that the terrible and furious adversary had crossed. Mi Pepe threw the rest of the fruit he was eating on the ground and followed after Coque.

They confronted each other face to face, kick to kick and then fist to fist. The fight was tremendous. My heart was pounding, I didn't dare to do anything, neither did my brothers, mi Pepe, so small, who after following mi Coque pulled weeds from the field and threw them over Rosell's head and face. Finally, mi Coque dodged two punches and with a single blow threw him to the ground and achieved his surrender.

From that day on, mi Coque was Tawa and mi Pepe was Etreuf. Later my Mánuel baptized a beautiful and obedient colt with the name of Tawa.

Tawa, the beautiful colt, was very faithful to my brother Mánuel, he would only allow himself be caught by him. He would offer little lumps of sugar and the horse would meekly approach him. Mi Mánuel was very disappointed when, after a vacation, his proud and spirited steed had become a docile animal and for some reason had been transformed into a gelding. Mi Papaíto, to my Mánuel's angry protest, alleged that this once spirited and indomitable steed was now only useful as a gelding.

Tawa coming to the defense the animals, the jungle, and the ecology (photo taken from the internet)

Worthy children

Three of them, the biggest, hid inside the irrigation ditch at five in the morning. They had the snares ready to catch the horses. The technique of catching the animals very early in the morning had been learned by my younger brothers. Zarquito and Pepe, accompanied by Coquito Gallardo, the oldest in this story, still only twelve or thirteen years old, had learned it from us, the older brothers. The youngest three, Abeto, Rafi and mi Cali were led by mi Chini.

They pulled a little woman and the three little ones away from the beasts in a corner of a large paddock. The idea was that, when the horses approached the irrigation ditch, the three hidden cowboys, with two or three turns of the lassos over their little heads, would catch the horses, stealthily roping them in a skillful maneuver that tossed the lassos over the heads of the obliging animals and wrapped them around their necks.

At the call of "let's go" the three riders launched themselves with the ropes, but they only succeeded in scaring the horses away. They only caught Blanquita, the mare of Joaquín Casas, the foreman of the Polloc ranch. The other mare, the enormous Blanca Luz was followed by more steeds that rushed at the children surrounding the place. The little ones raised their arms trying to stop the horses from passing, the little hands were raised 20 meters away, the little hands raised at 15 meters, with shouts, jumps and arms up, they tried to stop the advance of the animals, at ten meters the arms and the jumps became more energetic. Blanca Luz was implacable with whoever dared to impede her passage and hurried the zigzagging race, followed by more horses. The children were frightened and let them pass. This affront to their bravery angered my Papiancito and Zarquito, who shouted at the children, "What cowards you are!"

After more than two hours they only managed to catch Blanquita and an old mare named Chestnut. Although many other times they had managed to catch a horse for each one, this time six children mounted on Blanquita and the old mare, all in a line on the two backs, pulled by my Chini on foot, arrived late and jubilant for breakfast.

Milticepelec

Mi Chini inherited the red tricycle with fat, well-inflated white wheels. My new black bicycle with "balloon" (thick) tires could not compete with the agile bicycle of my Tiringo, which had been bought from Neto Rojas and took him round and round, following the bigger one, mi Mánuel's Goliath bicycle. Mi Pepe on his bright blue bicycle was trying to catch up with mi Coque on his red Garroso. The courtyard of the house at Cajamarca Street 628 woke up very early. The corridor around the pool, beneath the second floor supported by wooden pillars nailed to beautifully carved limestone bases, once again became a race track for bicycles, tricycles and dolls' strollers. Zarquito Balarezo played the role of strict judge and bicycle thief: every time someone fell off or went to the bathroom he would take his bicycle and ride around it two or three times at an impressive speed. His old bicycle was in need of repair.

The doors of the bedrooms, the living room, the dining room and the corridor leading to the kitchen, all around the courtyard, remained closed in order to avoid, not the noises, but the skidding and falling inside the rooms. The closed doors bore the stupendous figures that mi Delish had drawn on them. Those figures in chalk on each door paid homage to the members of the family: on the dining room door a giraffe and a caption that read: "*Jirafa Mechita.*" That's how mi Delish, so young, saw Mamaíta. She saw her as a giraffe. On the doors of each bedroom were drawn figures of my siblings and myself, with different nicknames that I can't remember. The figure of my father was on the door of the master bedroom: "*Capitan Gonzalito,*" read the caption, and there was a bull with a captain's cap. On the living room door there was a figure of a little goat dancing and a caption that read: "*Chiva Polita.*"

Tired of riding bicycles, and after jumping over several poles placed around the yard for playing high jump and obstacle courses, mi Mánuel, not because he was the only one who could read well, but because he was the oldest, and in fact the one who did it best, had finished reading "Tawa the Human Gazelle," and now could read the latest issue of Superman to us... If you are wondering why we didn't watch television, the reason is that in the early 1960's there was no television in Cajamarca.

So, at ten years of age, mi Manuel's reading was now better than it was years before, when he read us the Tarzan stories, pronouncing his name as "Terzan," which resulted in my naming one of my Polloc puppies Terzan.

Mi Manuel read it as "Mister Milticepelec" or simply "Milticeplec." But his name was Mr. Mxyzptlk.

He looked like a little man, an arrogant gnome, middle-aged, almost bald, gray on the sides and big-headed. He wore a little blue hat, with boots and gloves of the same color, and had a sinister, mocking and grotesque smile. He was a sly, deceitful, maliciously grinning cheater. The most horrible thing about him was that he was invincible, it was impossible to defeat him because he was so slippery. He was a little over one meter thirty centimeters tall and weighed less than thirty kilos. He could take any shape he wanted, but he mostly kept the shape of a prankster goblin.

We could summarize by saying that he was the mischievous and malicious gnome enemy of Superman, and he was worse than a goblin because he was real, he came from the fifth, or "Zrfff," dimension, and he came with bad intentions.

This capricious little man had magical powers that altered reality. It was not known how he came to Earth, to our third dimension. It was said that he crossed a bridge and had come to destroy the Earth, for which he would first have to destroy Superman.

His method was to alter reality. He would turn a simple rag into an elephant or he would make things disappear; he would alter the world by trying to throw it into chaos. It was not witchcraft. Milticepelec was not a sorcerer, he was just a hardened prankster with magical powers. He was, then, a super-villain, a court jester from the fifth mention who had learned to cross the gateway to Earth, and was therefore our enemy, a hated and baffling enemy.

The thing was is that Milticepelec could do whatever he wanted: he could bring a jar of water to life, or leave a fly motionless in the air, he could also make things or animals appear out of nowhere. If Superman didn't pursue him, he could become invisible or turn a stick into a huge snake that would defend him.

The only way to defeat Mr. Mixyzptlk was to get him to say, read, spell or write his name backwards. If he did so, he would immediately return to the fifth dimension, against his will of course, for a minimum of ninety days.

The trick Superman used to make him read his name backwards was to write his name in front of a mirror... What trick would you use? Can you say his name correctly? Let's see, what does it look like? Can you say it backwards?

"Milticepelec," the mischievous gnome, enemy of Superman (photo taken from the internet)

Diploma of attendance and assiduity

The previous year, mi Manuel had won a silver medal. To be more precise, he got the "first silver medal." The school awarded its best students at the end of each year: the student who came in first place deserved a gold medal, the second a silver medal, but if the matter was very close, or in an effort to stimulate the students, a "second gold medal" was often awarded. The same was done with the silver medals: if there was any significant dispute, first, second and even third silver medals were awarded.

Papaíto was very demanding as to our studies. He had been the top student in his school and was awarded with honors from the Naval Academy: he was a cadet commander at the end of his aspirational years. Lacking a good command of the English language, in which he had rudimentary classes from his teacher, one "*Pishgo Sattui*,"[79] in Cajamarca, he lost the distinction of continuing his studies at the prestigious American Naval Academy in Annapolis. Papaíto expected the best from us, his sons. He wanted to see us awarded by the school.

This year the award ceremony was held in the big hall on the second floor of the school. Paquito was a third grader in 1962. The ceremony was the same as always: first the children in the first grade were called ("transition" as it was called at that time). Mi Pepe got an "honorable mention," then the first graders were awarded. In the second grade my Coque, as always, got a silver medal. It was time for the third graders

79 A Pishgo is a species of sparrow – a reference to his birdlike appearance, Sattui, his surname

to receive their awards. Paquito was neither nervous nor confident, but neither was he excited about the grand prize.

Parents were called to place the medals around their children's necks. Papaíto had already awarded Pepe and Coque and was sitting in the front row. We third graders were standing behind the stage, waiting to be called, or not. Two gold medals, three silver medals and one bronze medal were awarded, and Paquito was not called. Papaíto's face changed from red and freckled to red and sweaty. Suddenly the presenter announced, "A special award is given," and held a silence that was imitated by the audience. "A diploma for attendance and assiduity is awarded to Francisco Sáenz Ráez," said the presenter and then a school assistant handed the diploma to Papaíto who took two steps forward.

My brown sweater with white edges on the collar and sleeves matched my pants and my shoes of the same elegant dark color, all gifts from my mother Delish. I approached my father expecting a kiss on the forehead, but he shook my hand and handed me the diploma with a look of uncertain satisfaction; the light applause was long overdue. Now I have no image of that past ceremony, I don't remember it, I didn't live it. My thoughts traveled to the stars, and from there to Polloc's horses and trinquitas races and walks with the dogs.

Later at home, my brothers Mánuel, Tiringo and Coque placed their silver medals on the necks of the statues of the virgen de Las Mercedes and Del Carmen that my abuelita Pola had in the parlor. Mi Pepe pinned a red and white ribbon on the mantle of the first virgin, he did it with a small golden safety pin that my Mamita Perpetua gave him amidst tears of triumph. Papaíto looked at me laughingly, and with a thin and mocking voice said: "Diploma of attendance of assiduity. Ha, ha, ha" and repeated: "Attendance and assiduity diploma!

Ha, ha, ha!" I never forgot: I never missed a day of school, I was never late. How great my attendance and assiduity diploma was. I will keep for the rest of my life.

Manuel Sáenz Ráez receives the silver medal, Félix Torrones Silva and Alberto Alegría the first and second gold medals

Beautiful pedigreed cows

We had spent several weeks without the presence of Papaíto and Mamaíta. That same morning they would return from their long trip to the United States, "*Los Staits*" as Papaíto used to say when referring to that admired and distant northern country, they went to buy cows, pedigree Holstein cows, three thousand dollars each. They bought about forty very fine cows. The total cost was approximately one hundred and twenty thousand dollars. With the cows came also a bull by the name of Willard, at the cost of an additional twenty thousand dollars. He was a beautiful black and white bull. He weighed about a ton, measured to the withers about three feet four inches, with symmetrical horns pointed forward, his appearance was that of magazines illustrating the Holstein breed. A ring adorned his nose, his skin shone and he was the pride of Polloc, although only for a short time because he died with a tumor in his chest impossible to cure. His loss was deeply felt. Happily, he left a son very similar to him, but of lesser breed (the climate of Cajamarca did not favor the breeding and development of fine animals). His name was Joselito. He was very cute, but a bit choleric. One day he almost broke the arm of an employee when he rammed him against the timbers of the corral door.

The cattle were imported through a loan granted by the Banco Agropecuario, which channeled money from the U.S. government, a so-called "conditional loan" to buy American cattle.

After transport from the state of Wisconsin to a port in the American West, the cattle were shipped to Callao, which took about thirty-five days to arrive. Once landed in the Peruvian port, a quarantine ("sanitary quarantine" it was called) had to be carried out. The cattle were immobilized for forty days to rule out any foreign disease or parasite. Once the quarantine was over, the valuable cargo was loaded onto seven trucks that departed from Lima and had to go to the city of Cajamarca; this 980 km stretch took three days and nights. Finally, from Cajamarca to Polloc over 30 km of muddy roads, the helpless load that we accompanied, following by truck in a journey of five hours, arrived at Polloc. The cattle, after this terrible odyssey, were exhausted and battered.

A ramp of solid ground was prepared at the height of the trucks' tailgates. We children were so proud and exhilarated. The trucks parked one by one backing up with their rear ends towards the embankment. My father supervised the operation, looking at the sky from time to time in a supplicant attitude. One by one they disembarked the animals with great difficulty. My father let out an enthusiastic tear demonstrating his crazy reasoning. Skinny, filthy, with their bodies bathed in feces, thirsty, they arrived at their loving destination, three thousand one hundred meters above sea level in the Peruvian Andes. The animals were accustomed to the warm stables of "Los Staits." Forty heifers had departed from Wisconsin, ten died in the sea transport to Callao. A total of twenty-seven heifers and one bull left the port for their destination, as three more of them had died during quarantine. Twenty-eight mistreated, hungry, weary and starving animals set foot on the fields of Polloc. Five others died in the first few months, only twelve or thirteen of them were able to produce offspring. Willard the big bull died due to a probable lung infection in the second or third year of his life in Polloc. The debt of close to a million dollars at the time, which included the construction of the stables, was the only thing that managed to develop.

Willard was his name, as yours might be Abigail, Tobias, Jonas or Catalina; you also have one or two additional names and surnames. The fine animals coming from "The Staits" also had names and surnames; Papst Willard Leader Comry was the full name of our beautiful bull.

Imagine that your full name is as follows: first, the place where you were born or raised; then, your present name for example Bernardo, Arnau or Francisca; then, your father's name and finally your mother's name. If my name were composed like this, my name would be Polloc Francisco Gonzalo Mercedes. What would you call yourself if we composed your name like this?

Certainly in Willard's case his name was composed as follows: Pabst, the ranch where he was born and raised; Willard, proper name; Leader, his father's name; and Comry, his mother's name; so his full name was Pabst Willard Leader Comry.

Three years later, in order to replace Willard, mi Papaíto imported another beautiful and fine bull by the name of Mayers Duke Orsby Fobs, but we simply called him Duke. The ranch where Duke grew up was the Mayers ranch, he was named Duke, his dad, Orsby, and his mom, Fobs... What would your best friend's name be if we made it up like this? Joselito, Willard's angry young bull was named Polloc Joselito Willard Trinny. Why do you think he was called that?

The end of this story is very sad: Joselito had no better destiny than to be embargoed by the bank, the Banco de Credito del Peru, a private bank that at the time leveraged millions of import debts. His departure was very sad: Papaíto ordered his smug animal to be taken out of the bullpen; one hand on his waist, the other holding his cap; his blue eyes stared at the floor, his face stopped doing what it always did: laugh; instead he bit his lips and cried. Mi Pepe, the only son who was in Polloc that fateful day, hugged Papaíto's left leg and cried with him. The truck departed from the north, bound to the south.

Willard and Papáito, late 1950s

The unremovable boots and the little smoker

From the trip my parents made to the United States of America, they brought us dark beige suede jackets as gifts, one for each of the male siblings. They had lambswool bottoms; they were very nice and warm. The little jackets were passed from brother to brother through the years that followed. They were very durable and admired by our friends. The best thing about them was that they gave us that touch of American western riders when we were on the horses, especially if we also wore the shiny brogue plaid shirts on our chest with the cuffs showing. This way we looked and felt like real cowboys; our parents' generous gifts of jackets and shirts were accompanied by cowboy boots, which were much appreciated by us.

The boots that our parents brought in all sizes given to the different ages of their children thankfully were made of leather. They had long narrow shanks, black leather soles and Nebraska pine wood heels, which on their edges sloped down to form trapezoids that rattled with every step. How proud we were of our boots!

The boots had only one problem: they were narrow. The shanks were bit tight, the toes were not. Made for slim feet like the Americans, the boots were not for medium wide feet like ours. This was aggravated by the fact that we Sáenz have concave feet: our insteps are angled at the top and the soles of our feet are shaped like the hollow of a hill.

Putting on our boots was a task that took us more than half an hour, at best. The shoehorns were too small for such long boots, so our toes were no help if we put them between the heel and the narrow shanks, which risked getting caught between the leather and the socks. More than once we sprained a toe. Banging on the floor or the walls helped the purpose of putting on our boots. Once they were on, they were tight for a few days, but after “taming them” they looked very good; however, the worst part was at night: taking off the boots was almost impossible. If it required the help of someone to pull them off. If that person was a small child, the result was unlikely. If it was an older person like Alicia or Herminia, the little ones ended up dragged along the floor. Only the strength of Mama Perpetua, Papáita or Mamaíta would make the blessed boots come off after twenty or thirty minutes of pulling with the children lying on their backs on the beds.

I wore my boots for more than a year, as did mi Ernes and my other siblings. Mi Manuel, arguing that his boots were too small for him, hid them from our parents, and then sold them for sixty soles. He did not only sell them, in fact it was a barter, because he added a pack of black unfiltered cigarettes of the Inka brand to the money received. The buyer was Pepín Pastor, a grown-up thirteen year old boy who introduced mi Manuel to smoking.

Blessed and praised

Pascuala arrived at the farmhouse accompanied by a dozen peasant girls. The arrival of Delishita to Polloc awakened memories of the times of my great-grandfather Manuel Cacho Galvez in the older campesinos. Their dark eyes brightened among all of them, rejoicing in the occasion. Dressed in long black suits that fell in splendorous waves of unfurling cotton fabric with every turn, they gave off airs of solemn joy. Beautiful, joyful and graceful, they sang to the "Most Holy Sacrament of the Altar." Though there was no Blessed Sacrament of the Altar there in the corridor of the house in Polloc, there was only my Delishita, loving, smiling and sure of what she was doing and deserved.

Colored ribbons were woven into their braids around their bronze-colored faces. Their cheeks reddened by the sun and the effect of the altitude of the Cajamarca Andes were highlighted by the white color of the long-sleeved blouses that ended in a myriad of colors on the cuffs. The small flowers, in their hair hidden by tightly woven hats, could only be seen when they bowed during the procession. The Blessed Sacrament of the Altar was the living God Himself, and His representative in the holy *agros*[80] of Polloc was, for them, my mother Delish.

"Blessed and praised be the Blessed Sacrament of the Altar," said the lyrics of the chants that continued in verses that I do not remember, accompanied by the harmonious dances of the girls. The image was marvelous, no matter how many times they repeated the same song, each time it was more and more beautiful and unique. It was 1956 or 1957, young Paquito was about three or four years old, the traditions of the hacienda in

80 Agricultural lands

the 1920s were being recollected, possibly dating back to the late 1800s. Pascuala came from Chuchún, where my ancestors' hacienda was located, near Polloc. There, my great-grandparents are more remembered. Delishita was considered as "*amita su merced.*"[81] Repeating this hundreds of times, they came to sing the verses of the Blessed Offering of the High Holy Sacrament, to remember, to magnify, to receive an offering, which, by the way, that time was not of great size or weight.

Young Paquito assessed the event, the details and its motivations well. In a moment of silence he said: "Pascuala, the Child God is here in Polloc," "Ay, amito, su merced," answered Pascuala, showing her worn teeth, and added: "*Dígaste,*[82] *amito.*" "Come all of you, follow me Pascuala," said the young Paquito and walked down the passage towards the kitchen.

Dressed in muddy leather boots, shorts and a flowered shirt, mi Ernes was in the kitchen, standing with a divine smile, blue eyes, light brown hair and a look of surprise. "Here is the God Child," said Paquito and pointed to Tiringuito, who didn't know what was happening. At once Pascuala snapped her fingers twice and the girls surrounded the beautiful child and sang: "Blessed and praised be the Blessed Sacrament of the Altar. Amito, my little child, my Little Child God. His hair of fine gold, my Little Child God," and the young girls, the *pallas* as they were called, touched Tiringo's hair. Pretty, they sang louder and louder in fine voices, and increasingly intoned the verse greeting the Child God. "His hair of fine gold," they repeated over and over again, touching his hair and kissing his hands, through which they touched the Child God himself.

---

81 Diminutive of Ama - Amo or Ama is a traditional title of affectionate respect given to a person in charge. Merced means mercy. The expression would be best translated "Merciful One."

82 You tell us or guide us…

The echo and tomato soup

I was very little, only three years old, I should have gone with Mamaíta on the back of the mare Primavera. Papaíto was riding Mensajera, mi Mánuel his colt Tawa, mi Érnes was riding Blanca Luz and my two year old Coque was riding in front of Papaíto in the same saddle.

The plan was to pass through La Quispa, where my cousin Mañuco was waiting for us on a beautiful caballo de paso; Uncle Leo on his horse named Frijolito, which, in order to show off, made it stand on its two hind legs; Aunt Delita and her two children: Delia Rosa and Leoncio, our very dear cousins, were also there.

My uncle Luchito had reinforced the road with stones to mitigate the mud and dirt on his trips to his hacienda. He had also set up two huge embankments that ran from one hill to the other in order to avoid having to go around twice. The rains in Polloquito, invariably every year, destroyed the embankments which Uncle Luchito, tireless, would build again. They came from the north and passed through La Quispa; sometimes the tremendous downpours flooded the pampas of Polloc. The roads for the vehicles, always muddy, made it difficult to travel in pickup trucks, but did not impede the passage of the horses, though it did slow them down. The rains of the previous nights destroyed the embankments so we had to go around the hills on a road that lasted more than three hours. Even so, our spirits and enthusiasm accompanied us all the way. The China Lindas – solitary and shy birds that are usually found alone or in pairs and flee from people – were eating the last remnants of barley in the well-kept fields of the huge Polloquito hacienda.

At eleven o'clock in the morning, as indicated by the shadows of the trees, we arrived at the beautiful house, modern and American in style. Built from wood, painted a dark lead gray, it broke the green color of the fields on the slopes of the hills imitating a silver mother of pearl. Framed in white edges, it stood out in such a harmonious place of green in all its shades. The white-framed windows and the gray roof gave a touch of solemn dedication. My aunt Chabuquita's good architectural taste was evident. Tío Luchito would have preferred the classic Spanish style in his hacienda house. With an extension of seven thousand hectares, Polloquito unfolded in an enormous and unforgettable landscape. More unforgettable, however, was the human warmth of the home, the house, the affection of my cousins and the warm tomato soup.

My grandmother Pola and Uncle Carlitos Cacho-Sousa ("Capish") attend mass at the Polloquito Church on one March 15th. The day of San José Obero, patron saint of the hacienda, late 1950's

That is how the caravan arrived at Polloquito and then, in the company of Uncle Luchito and my cousins Luis Manuel,

Tito and Potoño, who joined the expedition, we started the climb to the *jalca*, that is, to the heights of the peaks to see deer and foxes, to see the distant valleys of Polloc, to listen to the echo and to be closer to the sun. Aunt Chabuquita, little Mickey and my cousin Buca stayed at home to await our return.

It had taken us half an hour longer than expected because Uncle Leo diverted us on the way to Polloquito to see Chuchumarca Peak, part of his lands, and his rich discovery: the silver and copper mines.

The road to the *jalca* started from the hacienda house. We went in single file, the slow and rhythmic walking of the horses looked like a sacred procession: at the front of the expedition was my cousin Luis Manuel who, whip in hand, encouraged his horse not to be overtaken by cousin Mañuco. I could only look at the majestic Andes. From time to time my thoughts, to the rhythm of the horses' haunches that proceeded us, flew into fantasy.

The climb was not dangerous, the rhythm of the horses provided security. I remember the harmonious movements of the horses' flanks; the hooves did not slip, they gently pawed the greatest gift of the Lord, the land, the vital and beautiful land. Yes, we were landowners. My father and uncles were influential owners of extensive lands. They were fortunate heirs, but they were also loving fathers, hard-working farmers, hard-working ranchers, fair employers, borrowers in default, and value creators. They ate by the sweat of their brows, suffered from insomnia and nightmares, made the infertile lands of the Andes produce, hid from creditors and mourned their dead.

We reached the heights, but not the top of the highest peak. We arrived at the small esplanade from where we should be able to see the deer, rest our legs and kiss the sun. We didn't see any deer, nor rest our legs: uncle Luchito invited us to climb a huge rock that looked like a sleeping giant. Climbing up the stone exhausted our energy, grated our fingertips and left more than one of us with skinned knees. On the giant's belly, Mamaíta's baskets, and the one sent by my aunt Chabuquita were opened. In the first one, boiled potatoes with chicche (ground huacatay bathed in oil and salt), in the other Cajamarca cheese in small portions rolled up in slices of ham. We enjoyed the former with our fingers and the latter with wooden sticks with a sharp point at each end. To drink, the fresh water of the Virgin in our canteens and from the bottles that a black mule had carried to that place surrounded by the sky. An additional long stretch towards the heights exhausted the riders and horses. The reward was sensational: our heads almost touched the clouds, our sight was lost in the infinity, and ended in the *abra* (passage between the peaks) that awaited the course of the river. The river accompanied the whistling wind, demanding the attention of the angels who applauded us from the sky. How beautiful it was to be in the heights of Polloquito, without deer, without foxes, but with blue sky, green slopes of the hills, and the scarlet flow of the Polloc River that we saw in the distance on its way to the *abra* which hid the dwelling of the creator himself.

Uncle Luchito promised we would see foxes and deer, he also promised we would hear the echo of the hills if we shouted; there were no fox, no deer, there was no voice to answer our cries, maybe God kept those cries right there near the sky or, in any case, they are repeated in the echo left by these indelible letters of homage to the loving enthusiasm of my adorable uncle.

Taking a horse uphill is a simple thing: it goes slowly, you lean forward, you hold on to the mane and enjoy the swing.

What is difficult is to go down a hill, bad if there are several hills, worse if the horses want to return in a hurry, much worse if a rainstorm is looming. Descending on horseback exposes you to falling on your face over their necks and heads. You lean backwards and your feet in the stirrups is the only thing that supports your weight, it's worse if you don't have stirrups like me on the spring group ride, the descent squeezed my little body and my mamita's back that leaned backwards crushed me on the mare's haunches during the whole rushed return from our difficult journey. The animal that had no rider, the black mule, with a lack of weight on its back and no one pulling against the reins to restrain it, was the first to reach the house Polloquito. The arrival of the lone exhausted mule alarmed cousin Buca who I thought her father and brothers had disappeared.

The rain came after the last crack of thunder and lightning in the sky that had turned black, and the hailstones that hit our hats forced us to take out the ponchos that we were carrying beneath our legs and over the saddles. Wet, scared, and very cold, we arrived at our first return destination around 6 or 6:30 in the evening. It wasn't the strong wind that bothered us the most, nor our wet bodies and soaked heads, much less the fear of falling. What I remember most were the tremendous pangs of hunger and the intense cold, the few potatoes and thinly sliced ham were insufficient for all of the expedition.

The door of the house was opened quickly. The floors got wet. The ponchos were placed one on top of the other in a corner of the living room while an unfamiliar smell issued from the kitchen. The older folk sat at the big table the children at another small table. We watched as two pressure cooker pots full of delicious tomato soup came out. Its smell was unknown to me as I had never eaten tomato soup. I never imagined that you could make such a delicacy with tomatoes, a thick and delicious hot tomato broth. My aunt Chabuquita was the best of the out of that entire journey. I have a saying that I repeat when confronting any difficulty: "Neither the cold nor the onslaught matters if you can hope for some hot tomato soup."

Uncle Luchito and Aunt Chabuquita, loving parents of my cousin Chico-Sousa de Cárdenas, 1970's

The lady in black

Miss Filomena Llerena was a little old lady who always dressed in rigorous black from head to toe, a long cloak covering her head and hunched back, a blouse that we never saw, but could imagine, under the sweater of the same color, long skirt down to her feet, socks that we never saw either and shoes of old leather blackened with shoe polish. She would appear after the morning mass, at lunch time. My grandmother Pola received her with affection. She never lacked an extra plate, just as she never lacked one-and-a-half-real coins in her drawer to give to the beggars who passed by the house, hopelessly, on Saturdays at sunset.

She would carry a black umbrella to use as a walking stick, or occasionally as a canopy in a downpour, an umbrella that we never saw open, since she spent hours beneath a roof. Perhaps it could not be opened because it was old and battered. She listened to the seven o'clock mass in the morning at St. Peter's church, very close to her house. She had breakfast at my Aunt Bebe Rodriguez's house. At ten o'clock sharp she would enter the cathedral to pray the *Ora pro nobis*. In the afternoons she sat to accompany the Rosary that my grandmother forced us to pray daily, and from which we would sneak out once it was done, while they continued the "Pray for us" and the "*Kyrie eleison, Christe eleison,*" which were interminable.

In the afternoons, after visiting my grandmother, she would have lunch at the bishop's house next to the cathedral and then go to the church of La Recoleta. From six to seven o'clock at night she would again pray the Rosary and then return home. Her passage in the dark nights frightened the streets of Cajamarca, frightened the children, while the stones of the walls murmured: "There goes the blessed of the city."

Bored with the Rosary, we had no better idea than to hide the umbrella of the somnolent Miss Filomena. Very slowly, crawling, I slipped behind the kneeling Mamita Perpetua, Alicia and Herminia, who listened and prayed, convinced their wishes were rising to heaven.

I grabbed the umbrella and ran off in long strides. For my age of seven, I made a world record. Mi Coque and mi Pepe followed me laughing. Mi Coque tried to hide it behind a door and mi Pepe in a trunk in the small room, where we finally left it. We didn't know what happened next since, hidden, we fell asleep under mi Delish's bed. Miss Filomena came out that time very late because she had been waiting for the girls in the house to find her umbrella. This mischief cost us praying the Rosary and listening to the litanies for more than fifteen days; however, thanks to this occurrence, we did not see the aforementioned lady come to lunch for more than three weeks.

Church de la Recoleta in Cajamarca, where the Blessed Filomena finished her prayers, late 1950's (photo taken from the internet)

Harlequin, the horse nobody liked

My uncle Paquito, with his "great negotiating skills," made an inexplicable barter, exchanging his old hopper truck, a rickety piece of equipment, for two sacks of potatoes and a middle-aged gelding named Harlequin. He made the exchange just like that, without any further procedure nor time for discussion. He asked Papaíto to keep him in Polloc, so a corral was set up near the calf barn. Not much was expected from the gelding, perhaps he could work pulling a plow or with the foreman's supervision and surveillance of the barley planting or the new rye wheat that mi Papaíto had sown at his foreman's advice, but had not fulfilled any promise of profitability.

As he was not a horse that was loved or appreciated, the employees called him the insipid horse, apart from not being very beautiful, what caused them to consider him like that was that the employees actually did find him to be unpleasant. By Uncle Paquito's orders, he was not put to work, he was kept in his corral and only went out to be walked by a farmhand. He was useless for farm chores, he did not plow, nor could he be ridden for fun. We never rode him, much less the employees, and they had to take care of him and feed him without receiving any extraordinary gratuity; a gratuity that, I assure you, my uncle Paquito would never give, given his little-known generosity with money.

Insipid's presence and the care he received, since he had to be brought daily, in the morning and in the afternoon, to the grass that he ate with singular gluttony, did not make him a much loved horse. Nobody understood why that horse was not let loose in the paddocks, and even less, why he could not be ridden. His only merit was that he was not owned by Polloc: he was Uncle Paquito's horse.

Uncle Paquito's trade was often mocked and laughed at by Papaíto and the other uncles: a dump truck for only two sacks of potatoes and an ungraceful gelding was a bad deal for them. Even so, Uncle Paquito always defended his business negotiation, arguing that Harlequin was a beautiful horse and that someday he would win prizes at the national holiday fair.

Even though he was not very well provided with feed, the prohibition to use, ride and touch him fattened the horse and transformed it from a skinny and ugly horse to an acceptable steed. But it was not the love nor the lack thereof for this animal that was being taken into account, rather his high maintenance cost and low value.

The horse spent a few months in the corral. It was strange that when he saw another foal (an intact, ungelded horse) pass by, he became emboldened and tried to jump the fences of the corral to start a fight. This was not proper for a gelding, nor was it proper for him to fuss, lower his ears and raise his upper lip -and his whole head- when a beautiful filly or a fruitful mare passed near his corral.

One afternoon, Insipid escaped from the corral in pursuit of a black mare that was passing by fifty meters away on the road that led to the La Quispa hacienda. When the employees ran out to catch up with the useless horse, they found him in love with the mare, already having mounted the horse that had accepted the suitor. This news made Uncle Paquito very happy. "Harlequin was not a gelding but a very macho colt." his owner proudly stated with a huge joyful grin.

He left him with the long mane and bristled forehead that a fine Peruvian caballo de paso should have. He bought a saddle for him and hired a horse trainer; in fact, Harlequin looked completely refurbished, had a very smooth gait and moved with so much grace that we all admired him as he passed by.

Three months later Harlequin was entered in the most important fair of the region, the fair of the national holidays held at Los Baños del Inca. Harlequin conquered, winning the first prize among the colts of his age. This filled his owner with pride and boastfulness and earned him a long night of festivities and liquor. Even greater was the surprise and racket that ensued the following day when Harlequin was crowned as champion of champions among the colts from all the towns.

Within a few years, Harlequin had sired more than 50 offspring, his paternity was selling for many soles, and Uncle Paquito became known as a great negotiator and Harlequin went from being an ugly gelding to being a *chiclón* colt.[83]

83 Poorly gelded horse that has been left with an uncastrated (intact) testicle

Fox hunting

Struggling in our soaked boots and pants, we crossed the Polloc River towards the bushes and *zarzamoras*[84] of La Quispa. During the first hours of the morning we had enjoyed bathing in the river. The crystal clear water ran gently in the dry months, between April and November. Once the school classes of each first semester were over, we would go on vacation to Polloc; we did so that month of July with great devotion. The Polloc River traveled from north to south through the valley and disappeared in the Chuchún pass, leaving life in the fields and joy in the children.

Before bathing in the river we had fun riding the pigs that grazed nearby. It was fun, it was true, and it was fun to run after them, making believe we were riders in some circus or a Mexican or American western movie. We would catch up with them and with a leap, putting both hands on our haunches, we would land on their backs and the pigs would instantly pick up the pace and take us a few meters until we fell. If you fell on the ground rolling, your brothers would laugh but if you landed standing up and raised both arms towards the sky your brothers would applaud you and you would be consecrated as a rider or a trapeze artist worthy of admiration.

When the pigs fled far away from the river we dedicated ourselves to playing with cars, roads, tunnels, bridges and farms on the sands at the river's edge. The game consisted of making roads, farm houses and farms that simulated reality and directed dreams and illusions.

The trucks and vans were beautiful pebbles of all sizes and colors that we washed in the the river's abundant silt. I built a farm house surrounded by white pebbles, a vegetable garden

84 Blackberries

on the side bordered with twigs of broom, a slope towards the river, a small bridge and a tunnel under the sand. Small white stones simulated sheep; other black ones, cows, and those of different shades were caballos de paso and race horses.

My stone van left the ranch house, which I called "Beldad"(Beauty). My stupendous vehicle drove down the road, crossed the little bridge and then went under the tunnel. It set off to visit my brothers' haciendas; mi Mánuel's was up a small hill. The road widened and entered a field surrounded by corrals that each had, a medium-sized stone, of the same color, that simulated bulls in their boxes (corrals). Mi Coque decorated the entrance to his hacienda, which he called "La Biblia" (The Bible), with eucalyptus seed caps. That of mi Ernes, he insisted, was not a hacienda, it was an estate and was called "Navío" (Ship). On the roof of his house waved a little white feathered flag; the wind shook it, but the flag did not fall, it flew and got lost in the sky. Mi Chini made a little hut with twigs of the willow tree that gave shade and which we peacefully contemplated. He put many flowers and twigs in the center of a small square adorned by a pond. El Zarquito built an equestrian place which he described as a "haras," a horse breeding farm which he named "Éxito" (Success), foreshadowing his future. That of mi Pepe was the most beautiful. It was endearing. It climbed up a little hill that he said was called "Infinito" and the house, surrounded by white floripond leaves, let the sun shine through one of its little windows. The little hacienda was beautiful. Mi Pepe named it "Polloc." He built it to be seen at eleven o'clock in the morning and never to be forgotten.

After playing, contemplating and dreaming we crossed the river and decided to go fox hunting. The dogs helped us in that purpose. We advanced more than two kilometers through bushes, *aguajales*,[85] and zarzamoras. The idea was that the

85 Marshes

dogs would sniff out the foxes' tracks. We were afraid that the foxes would grab the dogs by the testicles, so we kept the males close to us and let the females run free.

We never saw a fox, only once we saw some small droppings in the mud that mi Manuel said were from a fox and that the dogs hated.

We returned a little late: in the distance we heard the bells from Polloc that surely Mamaíta was ringing for us to come to lunch. On our return, in haste, we crossed the river; the haciendas were all around. Finally, we all looked at mi Pepe's place, we contemplated it for a long time, and then we kept going promising to return.

The four little brothers Sáenz Ráez: Manuel, Ernes, Paquish, and Coque, classes over, eager to go to Polloc

Knock out, the girl boxer

"Quiet, gentlemen, quiet, gentlemen! Ladies and gentlemen: in this corner, Zorrito Herrera," said Gonzalito's voice. "In that one, Delita Sáenz." From their corners the two pugilists came to the center of the ring formed by a long rope tied around four sticks stuck in the ground of the big corral of my Grandmother Pola's house in Cajamarca, in the early thirties.

Delishita, at eleven years of age, dressed in small beige drill shorts, a thick belt sewn from the remnants of a saddle cinch, and a white cotton T-shirt moved her feet shod in black leather boots with such agility that she looked like a little grasshopper dancing over boiling water. In front of her was a sharp-eyed twelve-year-old boy, with a confident gaze fixed on his opponent's eyes, his heart beating to the rhythm of Carnival. From time to time Zorrito Herrera, so as to stop them from falling, would pull up his rolled-up pants – so loose that they seemed to belong to his older brother – up over his belly button. He did it with some difficulty because his hands were in big boxing gloves.

Papaíto, lacking opponents and taking advantage of Zorrito's constant visits, had no better idea than to challenge him to a boxing match with his little sister Delishita. He prepared his "stepsister" for this purpose with more than three weeks of training. Agility and accurate punching would be the key to victory. She would jump rope, climb the stairs to the second floor over and over again, and hit an old rubber ball stuffed with straw and sheep's wool that hung from the fig tree in the small corral.

"Boxers come out," said Papaíto who was, at the same time, the announcer, the referee, and Delishita'a trainer. The spectators: uncles Paquito Sáenz Cacho, Luchito and Carlitos Cacho-Sousa supporting their little friend Zorrito Herrera; on the opposing side: aunts Zurita and Delita Cacho Susa rooting for the girl boxer, while Juli and Jaimito, the littlest ones, who did not know what was happening, looked on, absorbed.

The fight began with Delishita dancing around her opponent, who, with his two little feet on tiptoes, gloves held high, and head and body feints, disconcerted his rival. El Zorrito tried to throw two punches in the face that were dodged by the boxing master in a very skillful downward twist of her body. Zorrito continued attacking without touching his nimble and agile opponent. Instantly, Delishita, in a quick fist movement, gave him a series of punches to the forehead. Zorrito, disoriented, tried to throw a hook that was also eluded with a jump backwards. Delishita continued dancing in circles around the kid, darting in and out accompanied by body and head jukes. Gonzalito shouted, "Jab, Delishita, jab," instructing her to throw direct blows.

"Attack, Zorrito, attack!" shouted Uncle Carlitos. "Serrano style, Zorrito, Serrano style!" harangued Uncle Paquito, causing Zorrito to leap towards the center of the ring. He put one leg forward, the left, and the other back about half a meter. The left arm and fist were aimed at Delishita's nose, the other arm held behind as if making a cross. The idea was to deliver a drunken Cajamarca punch, a right bomb-strike that would knock the opponent out of match. Zorrito's final move caused his rolled-up pants to stretch, tearing at the seat. He dropped his glance and his hand to feel the tear and in that carelessness Gonzalito's voice burst: "Now, Delishita, now!" she fired a right that sent the contender to the floor, knocked out.

The "you're out" was a disappointment for all the uncles and a joy for Gonzalito and his cousins. Delishita looked at her ex-opponent and helped him to get up with one hand. Zorrito's gaze was fixed on Delishita's eyes, troubling her, then

Zorrito said, “I love you, Delishita, I love you,” he was silent for a moment and continued, “Do you want to be my sweetheart, Delishita!” Delishita did not say yes, or no. From that day on Zorrito visited the house every day with great devotion.

The most beautiful child in town

The two children were dressed in short trousers with little heads of the same white color. Ernes was, because of how handsome he was, considered the most likely candidate to take the prize of the most beautiful child of the city. The contest was held in the fairgrounds of Los Baños del Inca in Cajamarca during 1950s. As young Paquito and his little brother Coque were still little brown eyed babies, they didn't have a chance in such an important event. Manuel, despite his beautiful light blue eyes, was merely a foil to Tiringuito (Ernes), after all, his chunky little body afforded virtually no hope for success.

The competition was very tight, many children competed in the occasion, and Mamaíta was very confident that her Ernes would be triumphant. When he came out on the catwalk carried by Mamaíta, the public applauded, the same as when other children appeared, carried by their parents and showing off their beauty. There was no way of knowing who would win. Mi Manuel paraded hand in hand with Papaíto, his short steps were very funny because of the movement of his chubby little arms and legs.

What was not taken into account is that the contest for the most beautiful and healthy child of the region, was organized by the Nestlé Company as a means of promoting its new product called Cerelac, which we liked so much because of its sugary cookie-like flavor.

Once the votes were counted, Manuel was designated the healthiest and most beautiful child in town.

Cerelac (shown here in its modern version) fed the healthiest and most beautiful child in town (photo taken from the internet)

An unforgettable visit

"*Peruanidad*[86] began when the first Spaniard went south from the island of the Gallo and set foot on these lands," said the enamored visitor who arrived that morning at my Grandmother Paula's house at Cajamarca Street 628, where we lived. The visitor was my Uncle Luchito Irigoyen, who came on his honeymoon with my Aunt Marujita to enjoy the Cajamarcan air and to show off his trophy obtained in the capital.

It was 1957 and Paquito was about four years old. The affectionate visitors convinced the children and the community that the best status for humans was marriage. Their nicknames were Chavalito and Chavalita, not only because of the hint of Spanish in my uncle's speech, but rather because of their love and fascination for the mother country. The first welcome reception was held in our house, which started with brandy and lemon water, later, when the smoked pork presided over the table, its mouth forced open by a very red and large Chilean apple, red wine in crystal glasses that my grandmother zealously kept in the oak and shiny glass cabinet located at the end of the large dining room was served.

We children were allowed to enter the dining room. The lustrous wood floors would not get dirty that time, or, since the occasion was of great importance, it didn't matter if the floors got dirty. The honoree and his new conquest were very remarkable, and with their words and gestures, they were sure to offer the gathering great lessons. Therefore we children should participate.

The words with which the couple were praised during the toast, to the relief of Papaíto, who did not like to speak in

86 Peruvianness

public, were pronounced by my Grandmother Pola: the sanctity of marriage was her main theme and the happiness of the bride and groom her primary prediction and wish. Then, as expected, it was Uncle Luchito's turn to answer.

Uncle Luchito and Aunt Marujita Irigoyen at the house in Cajamarca in 1957. Seated are Aunt Shurita, el niño Paquito and Delishita

Uncle Luchito's beautifully profound and unforgettable dissertation shook Paquito. "Holiness is a spiritual state, holiness is our goal, acts, not intentions, determine a man," The first part of his speech focused on values and holiness; "education and pedagogy must be a constant and permanent task, the important thing is to do pedagogy wherever you go and with whomever you find yourself." he said in the second part. Finally he implored that we love the homeland and know our identity: he vehemently affirmed that being Peruvian is a pride and that the Peruvian flag is the most beautiful in the world: the red of the blood shed by the heroes exalts us and commits us, and that the purity of the souls in the white must shine in the sentiments of peace and freedom. So he said and so I certify and remember. He ended with the prayer that he said was the most appropriate for the moment: "Our Father who art in heaven...," he continued followed by everyone and by the tears of my grandmother, the applause and cheers of the cousins, the memories for the children and the blessings of God.

The next day the celebration was at my Papá Manuelito's house on Amalia Puga Street, less than two blocks from the cathedral, people were lined up at the door to talk to the senator. The big news was the attendance of my cousins Cacho-Sousa de Cardenas, the children of my Uncle Luchito and Aunt Chabuquita, who were as young as we were. The lunch was magnificent, Papá Manuelito and Aunt Teresita presided over the table, we polite children sat at a side table while the grown-ups talked about travels and the welfare of the people; we children talked about horses, music and football, yes football. So chatting about football, we challenged each other to a match that was held right there in the courtyard of the house.

One team was formed by my cousins Cacho-Sousa and the other by the Sáenz Ráez; to reinforce the defense we chose my Uncle Luchito Irigoyen as goalkeeper, who generously accepted the invitation; to compensate for the help of an adult, my other Uncle Luchito, my cousins' father, who by the way would never let himself be defeated, participated as goalkeeper for the other team. I don't remember how the game went, I only know that we had fun and got so tired that all of us cousins ended up lying on the benches and the "bleachers" that separated the patio from the corridors. The only thing I remember is my cousin José Antonio (Potoño) standing out among all the players, to the point that he scored a goal from half-pitch and another one that eluded even the goalkeeper.

My cousins Cacho-Sousa de Cárdenas: Buca, Luis Manuel, Tito, Potoño and Mickey, a year and a half before (1956) at Papá Manuelito's house on Jirón Amalia Puga, Cajamarca

Polito, the pig who thought he was a dog

He was motivated by dogs; he thought he was a dog; he would go out with them when they barked at a visitor or passerby passing through the gates of Polloc. He would always trail a little further behind, because he could not run at the same speed and while they would say "woof, woof," he would say "oink, oink."

He suckled a dog from a very young age. He was given to my Chini when he was very young and she raised him with the same love and dedication that we gave to our dogs. Polito and the dogs slept at the doors of our rooms watching over our dreams and making sure we didn't go for a walk without them. They would run with us on our bikerides and horseback rides. We stroked them on their heads and fed them bran with skim milk or, in the absence of the latter, with the whey left by the preparation of butter, delicious and salty, which was prepared in the small factory that Papaíto had in his room at front of the south end of the esplanade of the ranch house.

Polito, the pig who thought he was a dog, was beautiful, golden with black spots, affectionate and playful. My Chini loved him very much. He was no more than thirty centimeters tall and would play fetch the stick with her which she would throw and he would return with in his mouth. He learned this from Campeón, Polloc's most outstanding dog; he also learned many other things from the other dogs: to chase cars, to enter the kitchen to ask us for food from our plates, to try to run after the horses in spite of the difficulty he had trying to run at the same speed as the dogs and horses. He always lagged far behind but this did not make him feel sorry for himself.

Polito, the piggy who thought he was a dog, made our lives happy. We loved him very much, especially my Chini who never had any other dog or pet, the dogs treated him like any other dog, without any distinction.

Upon our return from vacation, several months later, we did not find Polito at Polloc. When Mamaíta was asked about his whereabouts, she answered that, as he was very big and fat, he had been taken away by the canchuluc.

Months later, however, Polloc's cook, in a fit of frankness, confessed that Polito was slaughtered and made into chicharron during the carnival festivities. She also declared, with grief, that the diners cried at dinner and that not even the dogs wanted to eat the bones of their brother Polito, the piglet who thought he was a dog.

Green pampas, mountains of gold, ends of the earth

Juan Sin Miedo[87] was a very formal, brave and polite young teenager. He never disobeyed his parents. He never lied. This is how Mamaíta told us and this is how I want to put it in print.

Juan Sin Miedo, mounted on his horse, went with his two little brothers riding through the countryside and arrived at a creek between two rocks, the crystalline water flowed and provoked those with thirst to enjoy its pleasant and refreshing gift. While the three children were drinking the fresh water of the creek, an enormous bird as big as a stork and as beautiful as a heron, landed its white body on the shore. Juan Sin Miedo was an excellent hunter, he took out an arrow, aimed his bow and was ready in wait to kill the bird; however, when he saw such beauty and the deep and tearful look of the bird, he felt so dismayed and shocked by the candor of its eyes that he removed the arrow from his bow and spared the life of the beautiful flying bird.

At that very moment the bird transformed into a beautiful, slender, blond-haired girl, Juan's and the girl's eyes met and instantly they were in love, deeply in love.

"Beautiful boy," the blonde maiden said to him, "thank you for sparing my life, thank you for breaking the spell." She continued, "I am not a heron nor a bird. I am a princess who a witch enchanted and turned into an animal, but you have broken the spell." "I am happy to see you like this," said Juan Sin Miedo, "and I want to keep seeing you forever, to have you always by my side is my dream," he continued, to which the lady replied,

87 Fearless Juan

"I must go to my realm, my father, the king, is waiting for me there." "And where will I be able to see you?" added Juan.

"My kingdom is called Pampas Verdes, Montes de Oro, Fin del Mundo," replied the sweet girl, "and there I shall wait for you." Instantly the two young lovers looked into each other's eyes, without saying another word they hugged each other, committed themselves and vowed to meet again. The image of the girl vanished.

The three boys drank the water, filled their canteens and, getting on their horses, set off south, towards Pampas Verdes, Montes de Oro, Fin del Mundo.

They marched ahead on the horses for more than seven hours, two hours more on foot, pulling the animals along. Tired, they stood under a huge old weeping willow, identical to the one in Polloc by the river, the tree that lets its branches hang and kiss the water which flows along, crystalline. That willow in whose shade the little fish swim near the shore of the Polloc River. The weeping willow that guards the waters that provide drink for the thrushes and the Pishgo Indians; that weeping willow, so beautiful which rests and which provides rest, that cries and sings with the wind, that carries so many dreams, that dreams for so many days, that houses so much beauty.

The next day they were recuperated. After washing their faces, hands and little bodies (here and there) in the waters of this other river that was on their way, thirsty and rather hungry, they saw an orange tree, with ripe oranges, the color of the sun, so attractive that they were provoked. They plucked several of them, placed them on the ground and prepared to eat them, but when they opened the first fruit, a little voice came out of it and said: "Water, water, water." They ate the first orange, it was delicious. They opened a second orange and the little voice said: "Water, water, water," they ate it, though they were very surprised. They opened the third orange, which also said: "Water, water, water." Juan put it in the creek and they heard the little orange: "Gulp, gulp," and it seemed like it was drowning. The same with the next orange when he put it in the water: "Gulp, gulp," and again it seemed to be drowning because of the water. When they opened the fifth orange they were more careful. When the little orange said: "Water, water, water," Juan, with his hand, poured a little water on it and, at once, magically, bang! A fairy appeared and with an affable and satisfied voice said: "Thank you children for saving me, thank you for giving me water." The children were no longer frightened, they knew that a witch was out there bewitching people and fairies. "Let's go to Pampas Verdes, Montes de Oro, Fin del Mundo," the children said. The fairy gratefully gave them a knife, a piece of soap and a small grapefruit with water and immediately warned them: "These are magic things, keep them in case some witch or evil being wants to attack you." The children put the magical artifacts in their saddlebags and set off. The fairy disappeared.

They continued on their way, a steep mountain awaited them. The path was long, uphill and narrow. On the right a chain of mountains and on the left a huge and dangerous precipice. The agitated horses, step by step, climbed towards the peak of the highest mountain, the spirits of the two children and the teenager were getting more and more spirited, indomitable and anxious to reach their destination. They came to a bridge, a long bridge....

"Wait until they pass the bridge. In the meantime, go, children, brush your teeth and put on your pajamas and make pichi. Go, children, go. While the young people cross the bridge," my Mamaita would tell us, "and then wait for me in your beds." So she told us and we obeyed.

The tired horses finished crossing the bridge. The road got steeper. Suddenly some brutal wild boars with big bristle covered heads and sharp dangerous tusks began to chase them. They came closer and closer. When they came within reach, these hairy beasts began to bite furiously at the horses' legs and tried to chew the stirrups and calves of the children. They spurred the horses into a gallop and a run, but the hogs followed behind, increasingly more furious and vicious. Juan took the magic water bottle out of his saddlebag, opened it and reciting an incantation threw the water towards the sky. Instantly a rain shower appeared behind the horses and impeded the horrible wild boars from running. The rain fell and the pigs were left behind. "Giddy up, giddy up, little horses!" continued the boys.

After a few minutes the rain ceased. The capricious animals were again approaching. Juan Sin Miedo took out the magic knife and soap. He cut the soap into pieces with the knife, like scales. A huge patch of mud formed on the ground with the cut soap and foaming bubbles. The pigs slipped in the mud and fell into the abyss. Juan Sin Miedo and his two little brothers finally reached the summit, the top of the highest hill. They contemplated the beautiful landscape, from that part of the plateau, with such devotion that tears of emotion covered their faces. In the distance some green pampas, beyond them some mountains of gold and behind a rainbow of fourteen hues, the end of the world could be seen, the kingdom of their beloved and where they were almost about to arrive. They slept on the top of the hill...

"Sleep, children, tomorrow the story continues," said Mamaíta. So we went to sleep and awaited another day of fun and the following night for the continuation of the story.

When they awoke, three huge condors sat beside the children. A farmer had taken the horses. A page, who was also there, told them: "I have come on behalf of the princess to take you to the palace." Instantly the condors soared up and seized each of the boys by the shoulders and held them tightly in their talons, and, almost hurting them, lifted them into the air over the pampas and the mountains. The flight was long and exhausting, taking more than two hours. The condors covered them with their wings, protected them from the rains, but almost tore the skin from their shoulders. At last they arrived at the gates of the palace, a beautiful place adorned in mother-of-pearl and crystal. The gates were opened and they were taken to bathe, dress and to be received by the king, the queen and, of course, by the princess and other little princesses from the surrounding kingdoms who had come to visit and meet such brave travelers who had come from Polloc.

Thus the three little children visited Pampas Verdes, Montes de Oro, Fin del Mundo and were very happy when they and their parents also visited the place.

The girl who swept

That morning, once again, without any explanation, my little cousin Pili was sweeping the house. She swept all day and all afternoon, every day and every evening. Between the ages of three and five, my Pili was a sweeper. She would get up very early in the morning and sweep the corridors in front of her parents', Uncle Paquito and Aunt Mayita, room on the second floor of the house in Cajamarca. By mid-morning she would continue on the east side and, in the afternoons, after lunch, hurriedly, she would continue sweeping the west side. No one knowns why she was given to sweeping, perhaps because of the arrival of her brother Robert into the world, although that did not seem to be the reason, because since Fermín's arrival her little arms' and feet's eagerness to clean was already evident. The broom was bigger than she was, but she handled it with such dexterity that her size did not hinder her in her eagerness. The corridors were so clean that it was a pleasure.

The strangest thing was that, from one day to the next, suddenly and without warning, her desire to sweep and leave everything clean came suddenly to an end, and without any reason, this hobby, this illusion disappeared: on July 27th, after the school parade, she watched the children of La Aplicación (the children's school) pass by and for some strange reason, perhaps the look of a child or a mirage, from that day on, she unexpectedly never again took a broom in her hands, and until today, many years later, she has had no desire in the least to sweep anymore.

Two coffees for the head office

At five o'clock in the afternoon it is already cold during sunsets. In the sunsets of July, at five o'clock in the afternoon and without taking lunch, hunger arrives, always in those hours when the sun goes down.

How beautiful were the mornings and afternoons at the cattle fair at the Baños del Inca in Cajamarca during our childhood. At five o'clock in the afternoon, after so much jumping, racing and fun, we children were quite hungry, cold and in need of calories.

The Nestlé Company offered the visitors a free sample cup of delicious and warm coffee with milk. No matter how long we insistent children stood in line, the ladies would only give us one cup, which was very small by the way.

At the suggestion of mi Coque, we ran with Zarquito and Pepe, the four little brothers. Seeing that the microphone of the fair had been left abandoned in the middle of the livestock exhibition yard, turned on and ready to work, we approached very slowly and with a voice simulating that of an adult, in a serious request, we announced through the loudspeaker: "Ladies of Nestlé, please, please, two coffees to the commissary." The commissary was the place where the administrative offices of the fair were located. Our intention was that upon hearing the word commissary, the Nestlé ladies would take the request seriously. The plan was to place the order and run immediately to the commissary doors to receive the coffees.

We repeated the operation more than twenty times: "Two coffees to the commissary, two coffees to the commissary." We would say this repeatedly and run to the commissary. At the beginning we thought that the ladies would really take the coffees to the commissary, but that we were not arriving on time. That's why we took turns: two of us would order the coffee and while the other two would wait for them at the commissary.

It was about eight o'clock at night when Papaíto left the office and took us to the house in Cajamarca. There we realized that the ladies from Nestlé had never brought any coffee to the commissary.

Maritza and her daughters Marilyn and Marilú, and Tiringo go on a trip

When I was thirteen, I suffered a tremendous blow to my spirit. All of us little brothers suffered the same. Our Tiringuito, having finished his fourth year of high school, decided to join the Navy and follow the destiny that my father had so appropriately instilled in him. How we missed our Tiringo, oh, how we missed him! We would look at his bicycle sitting alone in the yard and cry, we would caress it and would clean it. I don't know if you know this, but traveling is like dying, at least the absence feels the same. Whoever leaves takes their dreams with them, whoever stays suffers loneliness and pain. Such is love, such is companionship; such was the love of brothers in Cajamarca.

As for me, I enjoyed running with my dogs, Baby and my Jet. I was excited to know that my little cow Maritza, the one mi Papaíto had given me as a gift for having assisted the milkings during the whole summer vacation at three in the morning without missing a single day, was about to give birth. The cow my Mánuel chose and received for the same reason never had a calf. I was very lucky: my mare China Linda and her offspring had already given me a troop of horses, my hope was that Maritza would do the same, and so it was. Maritza gave birth to Marilu and Marilyn and after a few years I had more than five beautiful dairy cows. But my Tiringo was no longer there. So I decided to study in Lima, to see him and be happy.

Tiringo went on a trip: Mamaíta surrounded by her children: Manuel, Paquito, Pepe, Abeto, Rafito, and Caly. Below "Baby," the dog given to us by Uncle Rafo Gómez

PART THREE

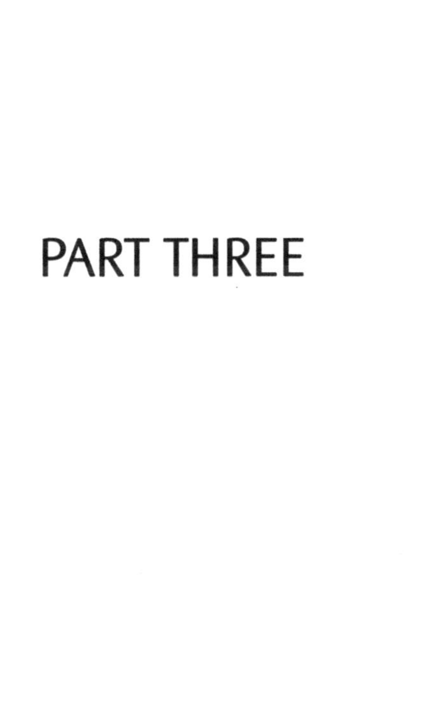

Boundless generosity

Acarosis is the name commonly used by physicians to designate the human parasitosis produced by the perverse mite Sarcoptes scabiei hominis. We simply called it "Scratchy Scratchy." These microscopic arachnids are parasites of animals and plants that, in various opportunities, such as the absence of hygiene, spread to humans.

A Volvo automobile pulled up to the doors of the Military Hospital early in 1972; two who were stowed in the trunk, five who emerged from of the back seat and three from the front, a total of ten young university students had arrived and were taken to get rid of the Scratchy Scratchy in the facilities of the only hospital that would accept them, since they were sponsored by someone connected to the place that was understood would bear all the expenses that the solution would require.

Having been infected in the UNI's[88] cafeteria among a thousand hungry students, scratching their shins for more than a week, insisted on itching, despite the many sores that burned, Paquito's ten friends got out of the car belonging to Uncle Jorge Ráez, a man of limitless generosity. Those attending the university dining halls were students of humble extraction who lived in the academic dormitories and who, when they languished, hungry, after the boring, incomprehensible and torturing mathematical analysis classes, went to the dining hall and, for a few soles, enjoyed a two course meal, a barley drink, a bowl of oatmeal with milk and a piece of fruit.

88 Universidad Nacional de Ingeniería, in Lima, Peru

My uncle Jorge's house in Jesús María had become, for quite some time, the usual place for my brother Tiringo to go when he left the naval school on weekends, accompanied by his inseparable friend Zorro Zambrano, and many times by a couple of other cadets. When Tiringo urged me to meet my cousins there weekly and greet my welcoming aunt and uncle, I was also accompanied by my friends Ramiro Leon, Ramoncito Anduaga and Miguelito Ortiz. My cousin Augustito Llorca also went there regularly.

The house of the man of boundless generosity soon became a meeting place for university students, naval school cadets, Cajamarcan students of all kinds, Ráez cousins, Saavedra cousins, Ráez Saavedra cousins and the Jewish friends of my cousins who became the sweethearts of more than one Cajamarquino. My friends would attend, encouraged by the conversation and the crushes of the cousins and friends, but mainly by the lunches, cookies and meals that Aunt Mayita and Uncle Jorge would so generously offer. We never perceived in them the least complaint or bad gesture. They were two angels who received us lovingly, givingly and accommodatingly. I remember that the large dining room table, which held more than ten people at a time, rotated its attendees two or three times each evening. As the years passed, when bonuses were no longer a novelty and studies were pressing, many friends, among them Julito Martos, continued to visit the house of generosity and friendship.

Many times I would go to the university cafeteria when time and money were at a premium. This usually happened during the third week of the month, when the allowance I received from my mother began to run out. The first few weeks I had lunch, when not at Aunt Viruchita's house, at the university restaurant where they prepared a spectacular "bistec con todo" (steak with everything).

From going to the university cafeteria I met several students who, in their busy student work, due to lack of water in the showers or other reasons that we will not elaborate, brought the "Scratchy Scratchy." For more than twenty days they had been suffering from this ailment and could not find a solution to their problem. The university had no doctor nor medicine to cure them and their poverty did not allow them to go to a private clinic; they only managed to ask for mercy from their friends who were a little more solvent and who attended the cafeteria. I had no better idea than to ask for help from Uncle Jorge, who, as we have already mentioned above, not only moved his contacts in the Military Hospital, but also personally picked up the students at the distant university and took them to the hospital.

Papaíto in a convertible jeep

BY MECHITA SÁENZ RÁEZ

I have memories of mi Papaíto from the time I was a little girl: Between the ages of three and five he would take me in the afternoons to El Salas restaurant in Cajamarca. Together with his friends, I would enjoy a rich white delicacy and listen to the long and fever-pitched conversations. I would happily lick my fingers with sweet pleasure, being part of a scene denied to my gender and age.

I would accompany him on his various supervisory visits to our beloved Polloc where he would give instructions, draw up accounts, check the condition of the cattle, and supervise the milking and the selling of milk. He taught me order, control, meticulousness, responsibility and, above all, kindness in the treatment of his employees, and the joy of living.

Those "outings" continued until I was quite old, because I also remember the mid-morning coffees at the Vichama Restaurant in Huacho, where I used to tell him my sorrows when my future was then destined to divorce.

In my adolescence, he never missed a ceremony or performance at my school. He never failed to drive me to classes, to basketball practice, to visit friends or even to *quinceañeros*. He was always there, supporting me, but also making sure that no one "dangerous" got close to his "greatest treasure."

Our talks were very unique because we thought completely different: we believed in totally different things, we dreamed differently, but deep down we both only wanted the best for each other. He never approved of my demands for rights similar to those of my brothers, my dreams of freedom, of wanting to dance, to go to parties, much less to travel. He was conservative and macho, his thoughts were confused between love and the desire to see me succeed. It was difficult for him to believe that a woman could be more than a housewife or an accountant's assistant because, according to him: "A woman should never go out in the street because, like fine silk, she wears out with just a glance."

My father was always a friend, he liked get-togethers, coffee or beer breaks or just to talk. His friends were of all ages. I remember with great joy seeing him at noon on a sunny work day in Huacho, and already at his seventy-five years of age, passing by in an open-top Jeep, standing up, laughing like a teenager. The Jeep was full of friends much younger than him, among them his cousin Pío Rosell, who were on a spree, probably on their way to some cheerful restaurant.

He resisted the loss of his ranch for which he had given everything. The loss of my Coque broke him down to the point of banging his head against the wall and crying like a child for hours. At times he was short of money. He endured blows and betrayals, suffered long and unfair trials and always came out ahead. No matter how much sadness his beautiful blue eyes reflected, he was there happily, inviting a beer, a blancmange or a coffee.

That is why today, twenty years after his death, I still mourn his absence. From heaven he undoubtedly enjoys seeing how far his ten children, whom he loved dearly and for whom he was capable of giving his life, have come.

PART FOUR

A FINAL STORY

The naval battle

He returned to his Cajamarca in 1953. He knew about compasses, stars in the sky and orientation at sea; he was proficient with the sextant and knew how to read navigation charts, his explanations of how to use the astrolabe were incomprehensible and he was an expert in measuring the heights of the stars on the horizon.

When Paquito was three months old, Papaíto went back to Cajamarca. He did so with Mamaíta and their three older children: Manuel, Ernesto and el niño Paquito. He took charge of the Polloc hacienda, beautiful Polloc... Do you know Polloc?

Obliged by family and hereditary responsibilities as the eldest son, he abandoned his brilliant naval career and took over the administration of the family estate. His mother, Grandmother Pola, and his younger siblings (Delish, Paquito and Julish), although already on their professional paths, rested all their expectations on the administration that Gonzalito would carry out. Since then, Papáito had two souls: one was in Polloc and the other sailed at sea.

The dogs were christened *Crucero* and *Fragata*, their children as *Corveta*, *Goleta* and *Submarino*. He bought a light blue Ford truck, which he named Huáscar in honor of the monitor ship that brought glory to Admiral Miguel Grau Seminario, the noblest and most dignified sailor who ever walked the earth and exalted the sea.

His office in Polloc had a large embossed oak desk that matched the small table surrounded by armchairs where he on rare occasions drank a glass of whiskey with an important visitor or, on very cold afternoons, drank a sage tea that warmed his body and calmed his nerves. This office was on the left hand side after passing through the timbers of the very large two-leaf gate that, at four or five meters high and ten meters wide, guarded the house. One crossed with a little jump over the trinquitas race course (the irrigation ditch) and, behind a light gray painted door that looked out onto the inner garden and the esplanade, to where one entered Papaíto's office. The noise of horses waiting to be ridden on the esplanade, which during some mornings or afternoons became a badminton court, did not distract him from his orderly accounting tasks or the recording of genetic and productive information of his dairy cows.

Crowning his space was a sword, his navy-grade sword with a golden handle and a silver-colored blade, which was encased in a black scabbard with golden ornaments. He guarded it with great zeal, cleaned it with shinning wax each week and then hung it on the wall behind his new cattleman's throne. The tables were adorned with replicas of warships and even a *caballito de totora*.

The walls and a glass case displayed photos of dairy cattle and trophies won at fairs and exhibitions of pedigree bulls and cows. To the side of his office, in a smaller room, he kept the reins, bridles, saddles and ropes. On a long bench, the three or four saddles gave a distinct touch to the place. The memories of the sea did not compete with the realities of the countryside: in a rare symbiosis they consolidated the personality of a cattle lover who longed for the sea. There were no awards or decorations for outstanding horses. Horses for him were only instruments of work and something that a rancher was obliged to have. His passion was dairy cows, bulls were for the same purpose and calves to be cared for. He never raised a donkey, a sheep or a pig, not even barnyard animals; these were all territory that Mamaíta had to exploit.

He was so orderly and scrupulous that in order to lend his small children a rope or a rein he made us sign "vouchers," which were actually recepts that obligated us to pay back the loan. He tried to run the hacienda with naval order. He hired a sergeant by the name of Joaquín Casas as foreman. In the mornings, this sergeant made the farmhands line up on the esplanade, he treated them in military style; the shouldering of sticks like rifles and the singing of the national anthem gave a touch of strict administrative management. They went out to the fields to start the work of cultivating barley and potatoes, pulling up the grass for the bulls, the cows and calves, and the alfalfa to feed the horses.

Easy to laugh, always a joker, protective of his daughters, a risk-taker in business and passionate about cattle raising and the navy. Once el niño Paquito, on the sly, climbed up to the window of his office to spy on him and saw him with the little ships playing naval combat. His miniature ships, the Grau and the Bolognesi, faced a huge squadron of enemies and won, not only by sailing, but by flying through the air and tapping the enemy ships. When he was at the breakfast table he would make little balls with bread crumbs, put them under one of his fingernails and, like a catapult that for him was an artillery cannon, at the thin voice of "pre-stop," "take aim," "fire!," he would shoot the little balls that, if they did not fall on the nose of one of his little children, would dive into the cup of milk or the semolina soup.

He liked to eat his soup with lots of salt. Every time Mamaíta served him a bowl, he would throw ten or twelve shakes of the salt shaker before tasting it and then drink it with great satisfaction. One time, knowing this custom, Paquito and his brothers, without him noticing, added more than twenty shakes of salt shaker when the soup was served. Papaíto, before eating it, as usual, added a dozen more shakes, stirred the liquid with the spoon and ate the soup with such satisfaction that he left the children speechless when he said: "How delicious this soup is."

He left us many lessons, with his virtues and his defects. Mánuel inherited his love for mathematics and the profession of agronomy; Érnes, his passion for the Navy and his full-fledged conservatism; Paquito, his jokes and courtship; mi Coque, his big heart; Pepe inherited his love for the haciendas and the nostalgia of living to serve. Kiko inherited his great tenacity; Mechita, his flirtatiousness and determination. Mi Chini, his optimism and devotion in raising a family. Abeto, his hair and forehead colors, the shape of his nose and his independent thinking. Rafi copied as if on tracing paper his bonhomie and his pleasant way of being. Finally, mi Cali stole his empathy and his serenity in the face of adversity.

His absence is not mourned because he lives on in each of the children he saw born. Mamaíta has the best memory of my father. When she surrounds herself with her children she feels the presence of fourteen souls, ten in her living children, two in her departed children and the rest in the soul of a sailor and a rancher.

PART FIVE

Poem for my brothers

Os lo digo como el gran Valdelomar: éramos doce hermanos,
¿recordáis?,
en el patio de la casa, ¿recordáis? Las trinquitas,
los saltos y aperis,
palos cada vez más altos y bicicletas daban vueltas,
¿recordáis? Quedamos ya diez hermanos, ¿lo sabéis?
Pronto seréis nueve. ¡No me olvidéis!

I tell you like the great Valdelomar: we were twelve brothers
and sisters, remember?
in the courtyard of the house, remember? The trinquitas,
the jumps and leap frog,
and bicycles went round and round, do you remember?
There are ten brothers and sisters left, do you know that?
Soon there will be nine. Don't forget me!

FINAL PART

The Characters

To help you unravel each story, let's list and describe the characters in these jokes. If you find it difficult to understand and identify each person in these short stories, I suggest you make a family tree on a simple piece of paper: Great-grandfather Manuel: Manuel Cacho Gálvez, the trunk of the family Cacho-Sousa. Father of Grandfather Manuelito, Grandmother Pola and Aunt Carmelita.

Great-grandmother Delia: Delia Sousa Matute, Wife of Great-grandfather Manuel. Mother of Manuel and Pola. Together with her husband the start the Cacho-Sousa lineage.

Abuelita Pola: Pola Delia Cacho-Sousa, Paternal Grandmother of Paquito, the Matriarch, love becoming life, Grandfather's sister, Mother of Papá Manuelito, Sister of Aunt Carmelita's father. Divorced from Grandfather Gonzalo, Mother of four children: Gonzalo, Delishita, Uncle Paquito and Julish.

Papá Manuelito: Manuel Cacho-Sousa, Brother of Grandmother Pola, el niño Paquito's Godfather. His children and grandchildren called him Payecito. First branch of the Cacho-Sousa trunk.

Aunt Teresita: Teresa Castro Agustí, Wife of Papá Manuelito, Mayecita, the sweet and severe mother of the Cacho-Sousa Castro.

Tío Alberto: Alberto Turpaud Cacho, Husand of Aunt Carmelita, both parents of the marvelous Turpaud cousins.

Turpaud cousins: Marisse, Jackeline and Mirelle Turpaud Cacho, Children of Uncle Alberto and Aunt Carmelita. Paquito's aunts.

Cousin Michell: Michell Turpaud Cacho, Brother of the Turpaud cousins, Son of Uncle Alberto and Aunt Carmelita. Paquito's Uncle, although he called both him and his sisters cousins.

Uncle Carlitos (Capish), Uncle Luchito, Aunt Shurita or Gracielita, Aunt Delita and Uncle Jaimito Cacho-Sousa Castro: Children of Papá Manuelito and Aunt Teresita, Paquito's uncles and aunts.

Aunt Chabuquita: Isabel de Cárdenas de Cacho-Sousa, Wife of Uncle Luchito Cacho-Sousa Castro, Mother of Buca (Isabel), Luis Manuel, Tito (Alberto), José Antonio (Potoño), Miguel, Patty, Alfredo, Juan Felipe and María Jesús.

Uncle Jaimito: Jaime Cacho-Sousa, Paquito's uncle, Son of Papá Manuelito and Aunt Teresita; Husband of Aunt Sonita and Father of Manolo, Jaime, Sonia and Sol Cacho-Sousa Velasquez, Paquito's cousins.

Cousin Pamen: María del Carmen Cacho-Souza Olivares, Daughter of my Uncle Carlitos and Aunt Mary, Paquito's cousin: loving, enchanting, happy and a fighter.

Uncle Luchito Irigoyen: Luis Irigoyen Cacho, brotherhood come to life, wise educator, proud Peruvian, Paquito's uncle

Aunt Viruchita: Elvira Bueno Cacho, loving aunt to Paquito.

Aunt Olguita, Olga Bueno Cacho de Amorín, enchanting and dear niece of my Grandmother Pola, Sister of Aunt Viruchita, Mother of Paquito's treasured cousins: Adolfito and Esperancita (Pelancha) Amorín Bueno.

Grandfather Gonzalo: Gonzalo Sáenz Zumarán, Paquito's Paternal Grandfather, Father of Gonzalo (Papaíto), Delish (Delishita or Mamá Delia), Uncle Paquito and Julish.

Papaíto: Gonzalo Sáenz Cacho, Paquito's father, Eldest Son of Grandfather Gonzalo and Grandmother Pola, whom is also known as Gonzalito or niño Gonzalito.

Mamaíta: Mercedes Ráez García, Meche or Mechita is Paqui Paquito's tos mother, his biological mother. Also known as madre Mechita in order to distinguish her from her daughter of the same name.

Delishita: Delia Sáenz Cacho, Delia or Delita, Paquito's second mother. Paquito called her mi madre Delish or mi madre Delia. Delishita was Gonzalo's sister, Meche's sister-in-law, Paquito's blood aunt.

Mamita Perpe or Mamita Perpetua: María Carmen Zelada Ordoñez was Paquito's third mother, virtue made human, a huge and loving soul. raised in Grandmother Pola's house from childhood, she was the nanny, called mamita by Paquito and his siblings, called Perpetuita or Pichucita by other family members.

Uncle Paquito: Francisco Sáenz Cacho, Brother of Papaíto and Delishita, Grandfather Gonzalo's and Grandmother Pola's, son Paquito's blood uncle.

Aunt Mayita: María Cristina Anduaga Pedraz, Aunt Maya, Wife of Uncle Paquito.

Cousins Paquico, Pili, Fermín, Robert, Elianita, Richard and Katia Sáenz Anduaga: Uncle Paquito's and Aunt Mayita's children, Paquito's first cousins.

Julish: Julio or Julito Sáenz Cacho, Papaíto's fourth son, Grandfather Gonzalo's and Grandmother Pola's son, Paquito's blood uncle.

Abuelito Ernesto: Ernesto Ráez Cisneros, Father of Mamaíta Meche, Paquito's maternal grandfather.

Uncle Jorge and Aunt Normita Ráez García: Mamaíta's siblings, Paquito's blood relatives.

Aunt Maya: María Cristina Saavedra, Wife of Uncle Jorge, Paquito's aunt.

Cousins Ceci, Genio, Carolina, Lizi and Jorge Ráez Saavedra: Uncle Jorge's and Aunt Maya's children, Paquito's first cousins.

Cousins Augustito, Augusto or Eustaquio and Luchito Llorca Ráez: Aunt Normita's children, Paquito's first cousins.

Neno: señora Lucha or señora Luchita, Abuelito Ernesto second wife.

Manuel, Mamuel, Mánuel, Mañé or Mañé-Mañé; Ernesto, Érnes, Tiringo or Tiringuito; Coque or Coque Panino; Pepe, Pepián or Pepiancito; Polita, Chini or Chinita; Alberto, Albertito or Abeto; Rafi, Rafito; Carlitos, Caly, Cuti Cuti or Quiti Quiti Cuti; Mechita, Mercedes Guadalupe or Pacharaca Ociosa, Fernandito and Enrique, Kiko or Kikirique: Paquito's siblings, Papaíto's and Mamaíta's children.

Zarquito: Zarco o Zarquito Balarezo Gayoso, Paquito's brother in spirit. Passed many long childhood years in company with Paquito and his siblings, loved as a son by Papaíto and Mamaíta.

Alicia: girl raised in Grandmother Pola's home, was the same age as Paquito's older brother Manuel, cared for by Delishita.

Herminia: girl raised in Grandmother Pola's home, also was the same age as Paquito's older brother Manuel, cared for by Mamaíta.

Paquito: Main protagonist of this work, main narrator. Son of Gonzalo and Meche, Grandson of Abuelito Gonzalo and Abuelita Pola, on the paternal side, and of Abuelito Ernesto and Abuelita Rosa, on the maternal side.

www.ingramcontent.com/pod-product-compliance
Lightning Source LLC
LaVergne TN
LVHW041020150826
845672LV00001B/157